All three girls jumped in surprise as a loud crash sounded from the hallway. It was the sudden, rattling clash of the front door being opened and hitting against the chain.

They looked at one another as a second crash echoed from the hall. Someone was clearly trying to get in.

Miranda sprang up from the couch and ran to the door of the lounge, only a split second ahead of Holly and Tracy.

As they stood breathlessly in the hall they could all see a hand come groping round the open edge of the door, feeling for the chain . . .

The Mystery Club series

Hide and Seek
The Mystery Club 7

Fiona Kelly

Hodder
Children's
Books

a division of Hodder Headline plc

Special thanks to Allan Frewin Jones.

First published in Great Britain in 1994 by Knight Books

10 9 8 7 6 5 4 3 2

A CIP catalogue record for this title is available from the
British Library.

ISBN 0 340 60723 8

Typeset by Hewer Text composition Services, Edinburgh
Printed and bound in Great Britain by
Cox & Wyman Ltd, Reading, Berkshire

Hodder Children's Books
A division of Hodder Headline plc
338 Euston Road
London NW1 3BH

1 An exciting invitation

'How long before we reach London?' Belinda Hayes gazed down through her wire-framed spectacles into her empty lunch box. 'I'm quite peckish.'

She had finished her packed lunch some time ago. Outside the train window the rolling English countryside glided away beneath a glorious blue sky.

Her two friends, Holly Adams and Tracy Foster, looked up at her in despair. She had been asking the same question for the last hour or more.

Tracy had been looking out of the window, passing the time by trying to count the sheep that dotted the fields of nearby farms. She rolled her bright blue eyes and rummaged through her bag, her blonde hair falling around her pretty face. She pulled out an apple.

'Eat this and stop complaining,' she said.

'I wasn't *complaining*,' said Belinda, pushing an unruly lock of dark hair off her face. 'I was just wondering when we'd get there.' She bit into the apple.

Holly, slim and brown-haired, tried to get back

to reading her book. It was difficult to concentrate with Belinda constantly interrupting.

Belinda nudged Holly with her foot.

'What are you reading?'

'A *book*,' Holly said with a frown. Holly was a voracious reader; her favourites were mystery novels.

'What's it about?' asked Belinda through a mouthful of apple.

'It's about this girl who keeps interrupting someone who is trying to read,' said Holly. 'I've just come to the bit where they go stark raving mad and throw her out of the train window.'

Tracy looked round at her. 'It isn't, is it?'

Holly laughed and closed her book. 'No, of course it isn't.' She looked at her watch. 'We should be at King's Cross Station in about forty-five minutes,' she said. 'Miranda and Peter will be there to meet us, if everything goes according to plan.'

It was an invitation from Holly's old friend Miranda that was bringing the three girls down from the little Yorkshire village of Willow Dale where they lived. Miranda Hunt and Peter Hamilton had been Holly's closest friends during the years when she and her family had lived in Highgate in North London.

Holly and her family had only recently moved from London to Yorkshire, when her mother had taken over the managership of a bank up there, and her father had given up his job as a solicitor to concentrate on his carpentry business.

Apart from her younger brother Jamie, Holly hadn't known anyone at the Winifred Bowen-Davies school. But Holly was quick-witted and intelligent, and it hadn't taken her long to set up the Mystery Club. The intention at first had been for the club members to read, swap and discuss Holly's beloved mystery novels.

Holly's disappointment that only Belinda and Tracy had turned up at the inaugural meeting of the Mystery Club had soon gone away when the three girls became firm friends and found themselves caught up in some very real mysteries.

But, as Holly had said to her two friends, at least there wasn't any mystery about what they'd be getting up to on *this* half-term holiday. They would be sightseeing in London and visiting all the attractions of that huge, exciting city. And to cap it all, Miranda had managed to get them all tickets to see a brand new musical, *The Snow Queen*.

'What's Miranda like?' asked Tracy. The plan was that the three girls would be staying at Miranda's house for the week.

'She's great,' said Holly. 'Really good fun. She was my best friend. Well, they both were, really, Miranda and Peter. Miranda still writes to me every few weeks. Peter doesn't so much, but then boys don't, do they?'

'I wouldn't know,' said Belinda, whose opinion of boys was that if they had four legs and a tail they'd *still* be less interesting than horses.

3

'Miranda's not one of these sporty types, is she? I mean, she's not some kind of fitness nut, like Tracy here?'

'I am not a *nut*,' said Tracy. 'I'm just not as lazy as you.'

Holly grinned. These exchanges between Belinda and Tracy were just another part of their friendship. Holly thought she would miss the sparring if it ever stopped.

'You'll like her,' Holly said to Belinda. 'She's a bit like you, really. She doesn't care what anyone thinks about her, and she's got a brilliant sense of humour.'

'Oh, no,' said Tracy. 'I don't think I could cope with another Belinda. One's more than enough.'

Belinda beamed. 'I think I like Miranda already,' she said, putting the apple core into her lunch box and sprawling contentedly on the seat. 'How long before we get to London?'

She gave a stifled yelp as the two friends dived at her and tried to cram her travelling bag down over her head.

There was all the usual chaos at King's Cross as the three friends joined the flow of disembarking passengers pouring down towards the ticket barrier. Tracy had two bags and a crammed rucksack weighing her down. Belinda had somehow managed to get all her things into a single hold-all which she was constantly having to apologise for

4

as it bumped against people's legs. Holly had a heavy shoulder bag and a suitcase. It didn't seem all that long ago when she had packed this same case with clothes on her travels away from London.

Slightly taller than her two friends, Holly craned her neck to see over the bobbing heads, hoping for an early sighting of Peter or Miranda.

She saw Peter first. Tall and skinny with a shock of brown hair falling over his eyes as he stretched his neck over the crowds beyond the barrier.

Holly waved and he waved back. Then she spotted Miranda's long corn-blonde hair and her huge grin and she waved even more frantically.

In another minute or two the five of them were standing among the flood of people on the station concourse and Holly was reeling from a violent hug from the laughing Miranda.

'Brilliant!' said Miranda. 'This is going to be a really great week.' She looked Holly up and down. 'You haven't changed a bit,' she said.

'I've only been gone a few months,' Holly said breathlessly. 'What did you expect? That I'd have grown an extra head or something?'

'I don't know,' said Miranda. 'Yorkshire's a pretty strange place from what you've been telling me.' She grinned at Holly's friends. 'Don't tell me,' she said. '*You're* Belinda, and *you're* Tracy.'

'That's right,' said Tracy.

'You don't sound very American,' Miranda said, looking at Tracy.

'You should hear her when she gets excited,' said Belinda.

'I'm only *half* American,' said Tracy. 'My mom's English.' Tracy had been living in England for three years now, ever since her American father and English mother had got divorced.

'Yes, yes,' said Miranda. 'That's right. I remember. Holly's told me all about both of you in her letters.'

'Really?' said Belinda, giving Holly a suspicious look. 'Such as what?'

'Only nice things,' said Miranda, smiling at Belinda. 'How's your horse? He's called Meltdown, isn't he?'

'That's right,' said Belinda. 'He sends his regards, and says sorry he couldn't make it down for the week, but he's got a gymkhana to train for.'

Miranda gave a startlingly loud yell of laughter. 'I like it,' she said. 'This is going to be fun.'

'I meant to warn you about her laugh,' said Holly with a grin. '*Loud*, isn't it?'

Miranda gave another laugh and linked arms with Holly. 'Let's get off home,' she said. 'We can start planning what we're going to do.' She looked at Tracy and Belinda. 'Have either of you been to London before?'

'I've been *through* it,' said Tracy. 'But I didn't get to see much.'

'That's great,' said Miranda. 'So there's tons to show you. What about you, Belinda?'

6

'I've been down here a few times,' said Belinda. 'But I've only seen the most obvious bits. You know, the Tower of London and Big Ben and so on.'

'Ahem,' said a quiet voice. Peter was grinning at them. 'Any chance of me getting a word in?'

'Oh, sorry, Peter,' said Holly. 'How are you?'

'I'm fine,' said Peter. 'But I'm just beginning to realise what it's going to be like trying to compete with *four* girls at full throttle. I've made a list of places we could go and see.' He pulled a sheet of paper out of his pocket. 'I've worked it all out on my dad's computer at home. It's all here.'

'Talk about organised,' said Tracy. 'Look at this.' She took the sheet from him. It comprised a long list of tourist attractions in London, divided between the number of days they were going to be there, and subdivided into the means of getting to them and the times that the journeys would take.

'I've made a list too,' said Holly, pulling the Mystery Club's red notebook out of her shoulder bag. 'We'll have to compare notes.'

'Hang on,' said Belinda. 'This is beginning to look like hard work.' She read over Tracy's shoulder. 'What's this? The eight a.m. train to Hampton Court?' She looked from Peter to Holly. 'You can cross that one out straightaway. There's no way I'm getting up that early. Don't either of you know what the word *holiday* means?'

7

'I know what you think it means,' said Holly. 'Lounging about in bed half the morning.'

'Take no notice of Belinda,' said Tracy, smiling at Peter. 'We want to see as much as possible.'

'They were only ideas,' said Peter. 'I thought it would be helpful for us to have a few firm plans to start off with. We don't have to follow it to the letter.'

'Thank heavens for that,' said Belinda.

'We'll have a proper think about it at my place,' said Miranda. 'Shall we go?'

They headed down to the Underground station, pushing their way through the milling crowds.

'Too many people,' puffed Belinda, following Miranda to the machine that dispensed tickets. 'What are they all up to? Don't they have any work to go to?'

'Mostly tourists,' said Miranda with a smile. 'Don't worry. It's only six stops on the Northern Line and we're home.' She fed some money into the machine and pressed a button. 'Keep close to me,' she said. 'We don't want anyone getting lost.'

'Don't worry,' said Belinda, stepping aside as someone with a colossal rucksack barged past. 'I certainly will.'

Holly walked happily along with her friends, remembering all the adventures she'd had with Peter and Miranda when all three of them had lived in London. It was nice to be back, and Holly was looking forward to showing Belinda and Tracy round all her old haunts.

Miranda lived in a tall, terraced house only a five-minute walk from the Underground station. She had older twin sisters, Becky and Rachel, who shared a huge attic bedroom. But the twins were away for the week and Belinda and Tracy were to have their room. Holly would be sleeping in with Miranda.

They dumped their bags and went through into the long, bright kitchen with French windows that overlooked a colourful garden.

'Your mum and dad are at work, I suppose?' said Holly.

'Yes,' said Miranda. 'Mum should be back from the office about sixish. I don't think we'll be seeing much of my dad, though. He's been working all hours since he decided to go on his own.' Holly had already learned from Miranda's letters that her father had set up his own advertising agency. Miranda's mother worked as a translator in a government department in Westminster.

Miranda opened the windows and they took cool drinks out on to the lawn.

'I'm completely free all week,' Miranda told them. 'Except for a couple of nights baby-sitting.' The ice rattled in her glass as she took a swig of lemonade. 'You remember Suzannah Winter, don't you, Holly?'

'The actress friend of your mum?' said Holly.

'Of course I do.' Holly had encountered Suzannah Winter a few times at Miranda's house. She remembered her as being very tall with long dark hair and piercing blue eyes. She also remembered that she had a little daughter, Charlotte.

'Is it Charlotte you're baby-sitting?' asked Holly.

'That's right,' said Miranda. 'Suzannah has got the starring role in that musical I told you about. She's the Snow Queen. That's how I've managed to get our free tickets.'

'Is it a proper West End show?' asked Tracy.

'Not quite,' said Miranda. 'They're staging it at the Hampstead Gardens Theatre at the moment. But if it's a success they're hoping to put it on at one of the big theatres in the West End.'

'I didn't know you knew any actresses,' Belinda said to Holly. 'Suzannah Winter? Should I know her? Is she famous? I mean, has she been in any films?'

'She mostly works in the theatre,' said Peter. 'But this is the first major role she's had for about six years, apparently. It's her big come-back after taking time off to look after Charlotte. She's got one of the cast staying with her.'

'Oh, yes,' said Miranda. 'Gail. Gail Farrier. She's renting a room in Suzannah's house while her own flat is being decorated or something. She's only got a small part. She's one of Suzannah's ice maidens.'

'What's she like?' asked Tracy.

'Gail? I don't know much about her,' said Miranda. 'She's very quiet. I haven't seen much of her, really. I don't think Charlotte likes her, though. Gail calls Charlotte "Lottie", and Charlotte can't stand that. She might only be five, but she's got very definite ideas about what she likes.' She smiled at the others. 'She's a really nice kid, though.'

'We wouldn't mind coming baby-sitting with you for a couple of evenings, so long as Suzannah doesn't mind us all turning up,' said Holly. She looked at Tracy and Belinda. 'We wouldn't mind, would we?'

'Of course we wouldn't,' said Tracy. 'We can't leave Miranda all on her own.'

'I'm not sure I'm very good with children,' said Belinda. 'I don't even know which way up you're supposed to hold them.'

Miranda gave a yell of laughter. 'Feet downwards usually does the trick,' she said. 'But it'd be great if you really don't mind. Suzannah's got heaps of videos we can watch, and she always fills the fridge with food and drinks for me. I'm sure she won't mind you all coming along. I'm baby-sitting Charlotte this evening. I'll give Suzannah a ring to make sure it's all right to bring you all with me.'

'I'm really busy this evening,' said Peter. 'I'm working on a car with a couple of friends.' He grinned ruefully at them. 'Sorry, but you'll have to count me out of baby-sitting.'

'Coward,' said Miranda. 'He's just scared of Charlotte, that's all it is.'

'Wise man,' said Belinda.

Holly stood up. 'Does anyone fancy a quick wander round the area? I can show you where I used to live.'

'I'll come with you,' said Peter. 'Then I'm going to have to head off home.'

'OK,' said Miranda. 'You lot go for a stroll. If you three get back here for about five o'clock, we'll have something to eat before going off to Suzannah's.'

Peter and the three girls headed off.

The main streets were busy and filled with traffic.

'Everyone seems in such a hurry,' said Belinda. 'Like a load of ants rushing around. And it's so noisy. Aren't there any quiet bits?'

'There are parks,' said Peter. 'And it's quieter in the back streets.' He shrugged. 'I don't really notice it, to be honest.'

'I like it,' said Tracy. 'It's lively. Like there's lots going on. Are you going to show us where you lived, Holly?'

They made their way from the bustle of the main streets into a more peaceful residential area.

Holly showed them the house that her family had lived in.

'I wish I could have a look inside,' she said. 'I'd like to know what the new people have done with it.'

'You're probably better off not knowing,' said Belinda.

A few streets away they came to Peter's house.

'See you in the morning,' he said. 'Have a nice evening baby-sitting, won't you?'

As the three girls walked away, Holly told them a few things about Peter. He lived alone with his father, who was a lecturer at a nearby college. His mother had died when Peter was very young.

'Poor thing,' said Tracy. 'I'd be lost without my mom.'

Holly took them on a long detour that she told them would eventually bring them back to Miranda's house.

'Is Horse Guards Parade on our sightseeing list?' asked Belinda. 'I'd like to see some horses.'

'We'll go through our lists this evening,' said Holly. 'Peter left his with me. Between us we should be able to sort out plenty of interesting places to go.'

'I want to go to Madame Tussaud's,' said Tracy. 'And the Planetarium.'

'Will we have time for the zoo?' asked Belinda.

'I wouldn't go there if I were you,' Tracy said, grinning. 'They might not let you out again.'

'I was thinking the same about you and the waxworks,' said Belinda. 'They've got a Chamber of Horrors in there. They might think you're an exhibit.'

'They do bus tours,' said Holly with a laugh.

'They even have open-topped buses. Perhaps we should go on one of those?'

They talked cheerfully as they made their way back to Miranda's house. The four girls had a quick meal before catching a bus for the short ride to Suzannah Winter's house.

Suzannah lived in a wide, tree-lined crescent of detached houses with long, elegant front gardens.

As they rounded the corner, chatting and laughing in the warmth of the early evening, Miranda suddenly came to a halt.

Further along the gently curving road a dark blue four-door car was parked by the kerb. It was facing away from them. There was a man at the wheel, and standing by the open door was a policewoman talking to another woman.

Holly recognised Suzannah Winter immediately. Tall and slender in a long black coat, her dark hair hanging halfway down her back, her sharply beautiful face lined with concern.

'I wonder what's going on?' said Miranda.

'There's one way to find out,' said Belinda.

As the four girls walked along to where Suzannah Winter was standing, the policewoman got into the car and it drove away.

'Is anything wrong?' asked Miranda.

Suzannah looked distractedly at them. 'Yes, I'm afraid there is,' she said, staring after the car.

Her piercing blue eyes turned to the four silent girls.

14

'Come inside,' she said. 'And I'll tell you all about it.'

They followed her up the path. At the door she stopped and looked round at them. 'They were looking for Gail,' she said as the girls gazed at her in amazement. 'They came here to arrest her!'

2   *The mysterious lodger*

The interior of Suzannah Winter's home was as
stylish as the actress herself. The four girls entered
a hallway with cool white walls and polished,
echoing floorboards.

Suzannah closed the front door and ushered
them into an attractive sitting-room of stripped-
pine furniture and Chinese vases with sprays of
dried flowers.

On a brightly-patterned rug at the far end of
the room a dark-haired five-year-old girl sat in a
confusion of toys. She had a rag doll in her lap
and was reading aloud from a large picture book.

She jumped up as she saw the four girls.

'Hello,' she said, running over to them and
smiling with curiosity up into the faces of the
three newcomers. 'My name's Charlotte, and this
is Polly.' She held the doll up in both hands.

'Hello, Charlotte,' said Miranda, crouching and
putting an arm round Charlotte's waist. 'These are
my friends. Remember I told you they were coming
to visit me? Do you remember what I told you their
names were?'

16

'*I* remember,' said Charlotte. 'But Polly isn't sure.' She lifted the doll. 'Polly forgets things,' she said. 'She's very old.'

Holly smiled. 'Hello, Charlotte,' she said. 'And hello, Polly. I'm Holly.'

'Holly and Polly,' giggled the little girl. 'You've nearly got the same names.' Polly hung limply in Charlotte's hands, her smiling face grey and battered with age, her gangly legs dangling out from underneath a crumpled blue dress. She had the look of a doll that had been the best friend of quite a few little girls down the years.

Miranda introduced Belinda and Tracy to Charlotte and Polly.

Charlotte stared in fascination at Belinda. Belinda smiled nervously back, puzzled that she should be the centre of the little girl's attention.

'Go and play, darling,' Suzannah said to Charlotte. 'While I have a quick word with Miranda and her friends.'

Charlotte caught hold of Belinda's hand. 'Come and meet my pony,' she said.

'You've got a pony?' said Belinda, brightening.

'Yes. He's called Sparky,' said Charlotte, pointing to a stuffed lilac-coloured pony lying on the rug.

'Oh, I see,' Belinda said, hiding her disappointment that the little girl had only meant a toy pony. Charlotte towed her across the room. Belinda knelt down. 'I've got a horse,' she said, picking the pony up. 'A *real* one. He's called Meltdown.'

Charlotte's eyes went round with amazement.

Suzannah looked at her watch. 'I need to be off in a couple of minutes,' she told the others. 'That visit by the police has put me all behind.'

'What did they want Gail for?' asked Miranda.

Suzannah lowered her voice, glancing over to where Charlotte was chattering happily to Belinda. 'They seemed to think that Gail was involved in something to do with selling drugs.'

The three girls looked at her in astonishment.

Suzannah shook her head. 'I'm sure it must all be some kind of mistake,' she said. 'I mean, I don't know Gail very well, but I can't believe she could be doing something like that.'

'What did they say?' asked Holly.

'They asked a lot of questions about her,' said Suzannah. 'Things like how long I'd known her and whether she had many visitors. I told them I've only known her for a couple of weeks. And no one's been to the house to see her.' She frowned. 'They must be wrong. She's such a quiet girl. They asked if I would mind them searching her room, so of course I let them.'

'Did they find anything?' asked Tracy, as intrigued by all this as Holly was.

'Nothing, so far as I could tell,' said Suzannah. She looked anxiously at her watch again. 'I've really got to get off to the theatre. Gail will probably

18

already be there.' She looked at Miranda. 'If Gail does come back here will you tell her what's happened? I expect she'll want to go straight to the police station to get all this nonsense cleared up.' She smiled at Holly and Tracy. 'I'm sorry about all this disturbance,' she said. 'There's plenty for you to eat and drink in the fridge. Now I really *must* be off.'

She said a brief goodbye to Charlotte. 'I'll phone later,' she told Miranda at the front door. 'Don't let Charlotte stay up too late. You know what she's like if she gets overtired.'

Miranda, Holly and Tracy stood staring at one another in the hall.

'Well,' said Holly. 'What do you make of that?'

'I don't know,' said Miranda. 'I wouldn't have thought Gail looked the sort to be taking drugs.'

'She didn't say anything about *taking* them,' said Tracy. 'She said the police were talking about her *selling* them.'

'I suppose it's possible,' said Miranda, glancing up the stairs towards Gail's room. 'It's creepy, though, isn't it? The idea of someone you know being involved in something like that. What do you think we should do if she comes back here? I don't fancy telling her about the police if she really is a drug-pusher.'

'She won't come here though, will she?' said Holly. 'She'll be at the theatre, like Suzannah said.'

'All the same,' said Miranda, 'I'm not having her just walking in here.' She went to the front door and put the chain on. 'There,' she said. 'At least she won't be able to get in now without us knowing.'

Belinda's face appeared round the sitting-room door. 'Help,' she said. 'Charlotte's talking me to death. What's going on?'

As they went back into the lounge, they explained to Belinda everything that Suzannah had said.

'Crumbs,' breathed Belinda. 'I hope they get her. Fancy Suzannah not knowing anything about it. You don't think she's got some drugs stashed away up in her room, do you?'

'Suzannah said the police already searched up there,' said Miranda.

'They might have missed something,' said Tracy, her eyes gleaming. 'What say we have a look?'

'We can't do that,' said Holly. 'We can't just go snooping around someone's house like that.'

'And Suzannah seems convinced it's a mistake anyway,' said Miranda.

Charlotte came running up. 'Sparky wants to play in the garden,' she said. 'And he wants you all to come and watch.' She grabbed hold of Belinda's hand. 'Belinda is going to make some jumps for Sparky, aren't you, Belinda? Like you said?'

'I'll do my best,' said Belinda, rolling her eyes as Charlotte led her off towards the kitchen.

Holly laughed. 'It looks like you've made a friend there,' she said.

Belinda poked her tongue out.

'I thought you didn't like baby-sitting,' said Tracy, as the three girls followed them out into the garden.

'Someone's got to put Sparky through his paces,' said Belinda. She looked around the garden. 'OK, Charlotte,' she said. 'Let's put a proper course up.'

They spent a while in the garden whilst Belinda constructed fences for Sparky to jump out of old bricks and flowerpots and bits of twig.

But all the while they were playing, the four older girls couldn't help but have one ear open for any sound of the front door being opened and Gail returning.

Belinda sprawled on the grass, having just taken Sparky on a clear round of the jumps. It didn't help that Polly was the jockey, and kept falling off.

'Any chance of something to eat?' panted Belinda. 'I'm whacked. That Charlotte's got so much energy. I can't think where she gets it all from.'

'Just think,' said Tracy. 'You were like that once.'

'I don't think I was,' said Belinda, watching as Miranda had her turn around the makeshift course. While Charlotte ran up and down cheering and shouting encouragement, Miranda made neighing noises and whoops of triumph at every cleared obstacle.

21

'She's crackers, isn't she?' said Belinda with a grin, as Miranda hit a jump and rolled with a scream of laughter on the grass.

'Just a bit,' said Holly. But she had something else on her mind. It had been running through her head all evening. 'Do you think Gail could really be a drug-pusher?' she said.

'I don't know and I don't care,' said Belinda. 'We're on holiday. The last thing I want is for us to get caught up in another mystery.' She heaved herself up on her elbows. 'Don't start *thinking* about it, Holly. I know you. Anyway, the police are on to her already, if she is. So there's nothing you can do, is there?'

'I suppose you're right,' said Holly. 'But aren't you in the least bit intrigued?'

'Not at all,' said Belinda. 'But I *am* getting hungry.' She sat up. 'Sixteen faults!' she yelled as another of the fences fell under Sparky's floppy hooves.

'I'm no good at this,' Miranda yelled breathlessly. 'Come on Holly, it's your go. I'll go and fix us something to eat.'

They ate out on the lawn while Charlotte entertained them with a gymnastic display on her climbing-frame.

'Bedtime, I think,' Miranda said to Charlotte.

'Can I have another aeroplane spin first?' asked Charlotte. Tracy had been giving her aeroplane spins until she was dizzy.

'OK,' said Miranda. 'One more aeroplane spin and then it's off to bed.'

'Wheeee!' squealed Charlotte as Tracy spun her one last time. 'Look at me!'

They went into the house.

'Can I have a story in bed?' asked Charlotte. 'Polly wants to hear a story.'

Miranda pulled Charlotte up into her arms. 'OK,' she said. 'One story for Polly, then it's straight to sleep, right?'

'Polly wants Belinda to read her a story,' said Charlotte. 'She told me.'

'I could go right off that doll,' Belinda murmured softly. 'I'm completely worn out.'

'Oh, go on,' said Tracy. 'A quick story won't kill you.'

'OK, OK,' said Belinda. 'I give in. If Polly wants a story then Polly shall have a story.' She lifted Charlotte out of Miranda's arms. 'Come on, then,' she puffed. 'Up the wooden hill to Bedfordshire, as my mother used to say.'

The three others went into the lounge. Miranda opened the cabinet where the videos were stored and they searched for something to watch.

'*Cinderella*!' said Tracy, pulling a video out. 'I haven't seen this for years. Come on, you guys, let's put this on.'

'You're so grown-up, sometimes, Tracy,' said Holly with a laugh.

'Oh, why not?' said Miranda. 'I'm too exhausted

to watch anything sensible right now. *Cinderella* it is.'

Belinda supervised Charlotte as she had a wash and brushed her teeth; then they went into Charlotte's room.

'Charlotte!' said Belinda in admiration. 'Your room is even messier than mine.' There were toys and clothes all over the place. Belinda was always under siege from her mother about the state of her room, but it was nothing compared to the chaos in here.

'We could play a game,' said Charlotte, picking her way through the heaps of her things.

'I don't think we can,' said Belinda. 'We'll get into trouble with your mummy if we stay up half the night playing games.' Despite herself, Belinda couldn't help liking the friendly little girl. 'Pick a book and I'll read to you while you're in bed.'

But before she would go to bed, Charlotte insisted on showing Belinda all her toys.

She had a row of piggy-banks on her windowsill.

Belinda picked one up and rattled it. A solitary chink sounded from inside.

'You haven't got much saved, have you?' said Belinda.

'That's not my *money* pig,' said Charlotte, lifting another pig and giving it a satisfyingly full-sounding shake. 'This is my money pig.' She looked at the pig in Belinda's hands. 'That's my secret pig,' she said solemnly.

'A *secret* pig,' said Belinda. 'Wow! Not many people have a secret pig. What's the secret?'

Charlotte shook her head. 'Not telling,' she said.

Charlotte delved into a heap of picture books and pulled one out. It had a picture on the front of a little girl being carried off by a giant eagle.

'Polly wants to hear this one,' she said to Belinda.

'OK,' said Belinda. 'Get into bed, then.'

Charlotte pulled the brightly patterned duvet back.

'What's that?' asked Belinda, spotting a small lump of something in the middle of the bed. She picked it up. It was a blob of multicoloured Plasticine. 'I'm sure you're not supposed to have *this* in bed with you. I'll put it with the rest. Where do you keep it?'

Charlotte clambered into bed. 'I lost the rest of it,' she said, pulling the covers over herself.

'Oh dear,' said Belinda. 'That's a shame. How did you lose it?'

Charlotte grinned. 'Not telling,' she said. 'I played a trick, but I can't tell you, or Mummy will be cross.'

Belinda nodded. 'I shan't breathe a word,' she said, putting the lump of Plasticine on the bedside table and sitting on the bed with the book in her lap.

'Right,' she said. 'Is Polly listening?'

Charlotte settled Polly down next to her in the bed, tucking the duvet round her. Belinda looked at the grubby old face of the doll, its features picked out with fraying threads. Black for the eyes and nose and a big red smile for the mouth. The doll's hair was tied into two straggly pigtails. It had probably been blonde once but was now a sort of grey colour.

'Polly looks very old,' said Belinda.

'She is,' said Charlotte. 'She was Mummy's. And before that she was Granny's.' She smiled sleepily. 'But she's *mine* now.'

Belinda nodded. 'Quite right, too,' she said. 'A girl's best friend is her dolly.'

Charlotte closed her eyes. 'You can be my best friend too,' she said. 'If you'd like to be.'

'Thank you,' said Belinda. 'I'd like that. Now then, what's this story all about?'

Downstairs Holly, Tracy and Miranda were sitting on the long sofa, handing round a bowl of peanuts and half-watching the cartoon film of *Cinderella* while they went through their sightseeing lists.

'If we follow Peter's plan we're going to need another holiday to recover,' said Holly. 'Belinda won't stand for being herded around all week.'

'You know what Peter's like,' said Miranda. 'He always has to have everything planned out to the last detail. We can just tick the things we fancy and ignore the rest. He won't mind.'

'As long as Belinda doesn't get away with spending half the day in bed,' added Tracy. 'You know what *she's* like.'

'She's certainly scored a hit with Charlotte,' said Miranda. 'Charlotte doesn't automatically like everyone.'

'Yes, you said,' Holly remarked. 'She didn't like Gail much, you said.'

'Children can be very perceptive like that,' said Tracy. 'The kids in my mom's nursery are very quick at deciding who they like.'

'Children generally like people who like *them*,' said Miranda. 'I think that's the problem with Gail. She's very stand-offish with Charlotte. I don't think she's used to having children around her.'

'How old is Gail?' asked Holly. She was still trying to form some sort of mental picture of Suzannah's strange lodger.

'Oh, mid-twenties, I imagine,' said Miranda. 'She's mainly a dancer, rather than an actress. A part-time one, anyway. Suzannah only met her a few weeks ago, like I told you. Gail was looking for somewhere to stay and Suzannah had a spare room, so she thought she'd help her out.' Miranda nodded thoughtfully. 'She's probably thinking that was a bit of a mistake right now.'

'I wonder how Belinda's getting on with her story,' said Tracy.

'Oh, she'll be up there for half an hour or so, if I know Charlotte,' said Miranda. 'Belinda will probably have to read half the books in her room before she goes off to sleep.' She grinned at the television. 'I like this bit,' she said. 'This is where that cat tries to catch the mice. I love the grin on the cat's face. It reminds me of— '

All three girls jumped in surprise as a loud crash sounded from the hallway. It was the sudden, rattling clash of the front door being opened and hitting against the chain.

They looked at one another as a second crash echoed from the hall. Someone was clearly trying to get in – someone who had a key, but who was being prevented from entering by the chain that Miranda had put on the door.

Miranda sprang up from the couch and ran to the door of the sitting-room, only a split second ahead of Holly and Tracy.

As they stood breathlessly in the hall they could all see a hand come groping round the open edge of the door, feeling for the chain.

3 Stranger in the house

As the three friends stood in the sitting-room doorway, the hand that was groping through the slightly open front door caught hold of the chain and gave it a fierce tug.

'Who's there?' shouted Miranda.

'What's going on?' sounded a woman's voice from beyond the front door. 'It's me. Gail. I can't get in.'

Miranda ran forwards. 'I've put the chain on,' she said. 'Just a minute.'

The hand withdrew and Miranda closed the door to disengage the chain. She opened the door again and Holly and Tracy looked with interest at the woman who was revealed standing in the porch.

She was tall and slim, with a neat bob of blonde hair and a pale, surprised-looking face. She wore a T-shirt and leggings, and it was obvious, even at a single glance, that she had the well-shaped muscles of a professional dancer.

She gave Miranda a puzzled smile. 'You don't usually put the chain on this early,' she said, stepping over the threshold.

'I thought you'd be at the theatre,' said Miranda.

'I should be,' said Gail, glancing at the other two girls. 'I got held up. Something came up unexpectedly. Are these your friends from Yorkshire?'

'That's right,' said Miranda. 'Holly and Tracy.' She looked anxiously at Gail. 'You haven't been to the theatre, then? You haven't seen Suzannah?'

Gail looked sharply at her. 'No,' she said. 'I'm on my way there now. I had to drop something off with a friend, and it took longer than I'd anticipated. Why? Is there something wrong?'

'The police have been here,' said Miranda.

Shock blazed for a moment across Gail's face, but then she seemed to compose herself. 'The police?' she said, her voice completely calm. 'What did they want?'

'Th – they were . . .' Miranda's voice trailed off and she looked desperately at Holly.

'They wanted to speak to you, I think,' said Holly. It was clear that Miranda was nervous about revealing to Gail the full reason for the visit of the police.

'Me?' said Gail. 'What did they want with me?'

'I'm not sure,' said Miranda. 'But Suzannah said that if you came back here I was to tell you that they'd been here. Suzannah thought you'd want to go to the police station and sort it all out.'

Gail ran her fingers through her hair. 'Yes,' she said. 'Yes. I shall do that.' She shook her head, smiling at the three girls. 'I can't imagine what they could want.'

'It was something to do with drugs,' blurted Tracy. 'They searched your room.'

'They did *what*?' Gail exclaimed, the smile vanishing from her face. She pushed past the three girls and ran up the stairs.

'Well done, Tracy,' hissed Holly. 'We can always rely on you to put your foot in it.'

'What have I said?' Tracy asked in astonishment. 'That's what they were here for, wasn't it? She'd have found out anyway.'

They glanced up the stairs at the sound of the door of Gail's room slamming closed behind her.

'Yes,' said Holly. 'But you've *warned* her now. If she is up to anything she'll be able to make a run for it.'

'We could always lock her in up there and phone the police,' said Tracy.

'Don't be daft,' said Miranda. 'We don't *know* that she's done anything at all. We can't just go round locking people up.'

'We'll just have to see what she does next,' said Holly. 'If she comes down with her bags, or anything like that, we can phone the police.'

The three girls were still whispering in the hall when Gail's door opened and she came slowly down the stairs. They spotted immediately that her hands were empty. And there was nowhere about her clothing that she could have hidden anything.

'I shall have to speak to Suzannah about this,' said Gail, frowning. 'Letting people go through my things without my permission. It's not right.'

'Perhaps if you go to the police station?' suggested Holly.

'I certainly shall,' Gail said angrily. 'Don't worry about that. This is an invasion of privacy. I don't know anything about any drugs.'

'It was probably a case of mistaken identity,' Tracy said hopefully. 'You probably *look* like someone they were after.'

'Yes. Possibly,' said Gail. 'But that's no excuse.' She looked at her watch. 'I'm too late for the performance now, anyway,' she said. 'They'll have got an understudy to fill in for me. I suppose I'd better get off to the police station.' She smiled at the three girls. 'I'm sorry about this,' she said. 'You get back to whatever you were doing. Is Lottie in bed yet?'

'Yes,' said Miranda.

Gail walked into the sitting-room, hearing the sound of the video film. '*Cinderella*,' she said. 'I always preferred *Snow White*, myself. You carry on watching it.' She walked along the room. She looked as if she was searching for something. By the rug where a few of Charlotte's toys were still scattered, she turned, seeing that the girls were still standing watching her.

'Have you lost something?' asked Miranda.

'No,' said Gail. 'I was just . . .' Her voice trailed off and she smiled again. Holly got the

32

definite impression that the smile was something of a strain.

'I've just got to fetch something from upstairs,' said Gail. 'Then I'll go straight to the police station.'

After she had left the sitting-room the three girls gathered to whisper together.

'Keep an eye on her when she comes back down,' said Miranda. 'If she's got anything with her we'll call the police, right?'

'I still think we should lock her up and *then* call the police,' said Tracy.

'I wouldn't try it,' said Miranda. 'She may not look it, but she's very strong. I wouldn't want to get into a fight with her.'

'Let's just leave the door open,' said Holly. 'That way we can see her as she goes past. If she's carrying *anything*, we'll call the police.'

The three girls stood silently by the open sitting-room door, waiting with bated breath for Gail to come back down again.

Belinda winced as she heard the clatter of the front door come echoing up the stairs. Charlotte had finally closed her eyes only a few minutes previously, and Belinda was on her third story.

She expected to see the child's dark eyes flutter open. If this kept up she'd be reading stories until midnight.

But Charlotte didn't seem to hear the noise.

Perhaps, Belinda thought, she really had finally gone to sleep. She carried on reading just to be on the safe side, edging her way cautiously to the end of the bed so that she could make her escape without disturbing Charlotte.

In the background, behind the sound of her own voice, she heard someone come up the stairs and enter a nearby room. The door slammed and Charlotte's head turned and she murmured something. But her eyes didn't open.

Belinda wanted to be out there. She wanted to know what was going on. A few seconds elapsed and she heard whoever it was go back downstairs.

Belinda waited for a few moments, then stood up and closed the book. Charlotte didn't move.

Belinda grinned and tiptoed to the door. It suddenly occurred to her to close the curtains and she was picking her way cautiously across the muddle on the floor when she heard feet on the stairs again.

She paused as she heard the footsteps stop outside Charlotte's bedroom door. She turned and looked round as she saw the door edge open.

The face of an unknown blonde woman appeared in the crack. But the surprised expression on Belinda's face was nothing compared to the startled look that the woman gave her when she saw Belinda standing there.

Belinda put her finger to her lips and crept back

to the door. The woman backed into the hall as Belinda closed the door behind them.

'She's just dropped off,' said Belinda. 'Are you Gail?'

The woman nodded. 'I just looked in to say goodnight to her,' said Gail.

Belinda shook her head. 'I don't think you should disturb her,' she said. 'It's taken me half an hour to get her off.'

Gail stared at the closed door. 'No,' she said. 'I suppose you're right. I'd better not.'

'Have the others told you everything?' asked Belinda.

Gail nodded and went into her room, unable to hide the anxiety on her face.

Belinda was about to go downstairs when Charlotte's door opened from the inside.

'You didn't finish the story,' said Charlotte, blinking sleepily at Belinda.

'You little monkey,' said Belinda with a grin. 'I thought you were asleep.'

'I woke up,' murmured Charlotte.

'Come on, then,' said Belinda. 'Back you go. I'll finish the story, and then you've really got to go to sleep.' As she closed the door she heard Gail come out of her own room and go downstairs.

Gail looked at the three girls standing in the sitting-room doorway. 'Not watching your video?' she said.

'We were just going to get ourselves something to eat,' Miranda said quickly. 'Do you want me to give a message to Suzannah if she gets back before you?'

'Just tell her I've gone to the police to sort everything out,' said Gail. 'Tell her not to worry about it.'

As before, the three girls could see no sign that Gail had brought anything down with her.

She left the house.

'Well?' said Holly. 'Do you think she's really going to the police?'

'She didn't have anything with her,' said Miranda. 'If she has got drugs hidden up there, I don't see how she could have smuggled them past without us seeing. I think we ought to believe her.'

Tracy and Holly nodded. There really didn't seem anything else to do.

'Let's close these curtains,' said Belinda as Charlotte snuggled up under the duvet. 'Then I'll finish your story.'

She glanced out of the window. In the evening light she could clearly see down into the wide street. Just as she was about to draw the curtains she heard the front door close. She peered down and saw Gail walk rapidly across the road.

Belinda's eyes widened and she caught her breath. Parked a little way along the road on the far side, was a car that looked exactly the same as the one the police had driven off in earlier that evening. A dark blue four-door car. But it was too far away for Belinda to be able to read the number plates.

Gail headed straight for the car. The driver's door opened and Belinda saw Gail lean over and talk to someone inside. A third person was sitting in the front passenger seat, but the car was too far away for Belinda even to tell if it was a man or a woman. It was just a dark shape through the window.

Gail was gesturing towards the house and shaking her head. And then Gail stepped back from the car as if something had startled her. She looked for a moment as if she was going to run, but then the person she had been speaking to got out of the car and caught hold of her arm.

It was a man. A short, stocky man with dark hair and a brown leather jacket. He spoke to Gail for a few moments then released her. Gail held her hands out in a placating gesture and opened the back door of the car. Whatever he had said to her had obviously convinced her to go with them.

They both got into the car. The engine started and the car headed off down the crescent.

Belinda stood, frowning, at the window for a moment, wondering what was going on. She drew the curtains closed and looked round.

She smiled. Charlotte's head was on her pillow and her eyes were closed. It didn't look as if Belinda was going to have to finish the story after all. She crept past the sleeping child and made her way downstairs.

'What was all that about?' she asked the others.

They told her what had happened.

'Gail said she's going straight to the police,' said Holly.

'Did she now?' said Belinda. 'That's odd. Because I've just seen her getting into a car that looked remarkably like the one that the police were in earlier.' She looked meaningfully at her three friends. 'In fact, I'd be prepared to swear in court it was the same one. What do you make of that?'

The four girls were still puzzling over this curious incident when the phone rang and Miranda went to answer it.

'It was a message from Suzannah,' she told the others after she had put the receiver down. 'She's going to be a lot later than she thought. There's some important meeting taking place after the show tonight. She's not going to be back before midnight, she doesn't think.'

'Did you tell her about Gail?' asked Holly.

'No,' said Miranda. 'It wasn't Suzannah on the phone. It was one of the backstage people who help in her dressing-room. But Suzannah asked if we could possibly stay the night.' Miranda sat on the arm of the sofa. 'This does happen sometimes – Suzannah being later than she expects – but usually Mrs Taylor from down the road takes Charlotte. Only Mrs Taylor wasn't at home when they phoned.' Miranda shrugged. 'I'll stay, of course, but you three can go back to my place if you prefer.'

'I think we'd rather stay here with you,' said Holly. 'If there are enough places for us to sleep.'

Miranda smiled in relief. 'There's a spare bedroom that will hold a couple of us. I can sleep in with Charlotte. And one of us can sleep on the sofa in here. I'll just phone home and let them know what's going on.'

While Miranda was on the phone, the other three girls tossed coins for who would sleep on the sofa.

'Typical,' said Holly, looking down at the coin that had lost her the chance of a proper bed. 'I'm the tallest one and I get the sofa.'

'I don't mind swapping,' said Tracy. 'I've got to sleep with Belinda and she snores.'

'I do *not* snore,' Belinda said, affronted. 'And at least I don't talk in my sleep like some people I could mention.'

'*Excuse* me,' said Tracy. 'I do not talk in my sleep.'

'Yes, you do,' insisted Belinda. 'It's like trying to get to sleep with the radio on.'

Holly laughed. 'It sounds like I'll be better off on the sofa after all,' she said. She glanced round as Miranda came back into the room.

'It's all fixed,' said Miranda. 'Mum and Dad are quite happy about us staying over here. Shall we get ourselves a bit of supper and finish watching *Cinderella*?'

It was quite late before the four girls finally succumbed to tiredness and started preparing for bed.

The puzzle of Gail's behaviour had kept them talking all evening. Had it been the police car that Belinda had seen? Or – as Tracy suggested – did Belinda's glasses need a good clean? In the end they had given up, perplexed.

'I'd better leave the chain off,' said Miranda. 'Gail will be back at some stage, I suppose. And Suzannah will want to get in anyway.'

'And with any luck we'll find out in the morning exactly what's going on,' Holly said with a yawn.

They found her some blankets and she spread them out on the sofa.

Holly switched the light off and half-undressed, listening to the quiet sounds of her three friends going up to bed.

She plumped up a couple of cushions for pillows and tried to make herself comfortable on the sofa. It wasn't easy. The sofa wasn't long enough for her to stretch out without propping her feet up on the arm, and that wasn't comfortable for more than two minutes.

She curled up on her side, drawing her legs up.

Half an hour later she was still awake and beginning to wish she had accepted Tracy's offer. Even if Belinda did snore, it would be better than this.

She turned over and felt a draught on her back where the blankets had pulled away. She sat up in the darkness and tried to rearrange her bedding. A clock was ticking slowly away to itself on the mantelpiece, but it was too dark for Holly to see the time.

She was just reaching for her watch when she heard a sound.

A very stealthy sound. Magnified by the general silence.

The sound of a key in the lock of the front door.

It must be Gail coming back, she thought, *or possibly Suzannah.*

Holly listened intently, hearing the front door creak softly open. She watched the bottom of the sitting-room door, waiting for the strip of light that would show that the hall light had been put on.

Footsteps clicked slowly on the floorboards. Whoever it was, they were being very quiet. And they hadn't put the light on.

Holly frowned. Neither had they closed the front door behind them.

A sudden thought struck her. Was it Gail? Had she come back for whatever she hadn't dared to take from the house with the three of them watching her?

Holly slipped her skirt on and padded to the sitting-room door, her heart beating wildly.

She took a deep, steadying breath and opened the door.

Standing at the foot of the stairs in the gloom, one hand poised on the banister rail, was a woman that Holly had never seen before in her life. A woman with cropped dark brown hair, wearing a brown leather jacket and faded black jeans.

Not Gail, and certainly not Suzannah. A complete stranger, lifting one silent foot to the first stair tread.

The woman's head snapped round, and the expression of angry shock on her face as she glared at her almost stopped Holly's thudding heart.

4 Lost at the fair

Holly gasped as the strange woman's gaze bored into her. Holly was too startled even to shout, but the woman recovered herself quickly. She darted towards Holly, pushing her off-balance back into the darkened lounge. Even as Holly tripped and fell, she heard the woman's feet clatter down the long path.

Holly sprang up and ran to the open front door.

'Stop!' she yelled, seeing the dark shadow of the woman running along the pavement. A car door opened and the woman scrambled in as it sped away, the door swinging open for a moment before a hand came out to slam it shut.

Holly closed the front door. It would have been pointless to try and follow. The car was driving away and it was far too dark for her to have seen anything.

A face appeared at the top of the stairs. It was Miranda.

'What's happened?'

'There was a woman,' said Holly. 'A strange woman in the house.'

Miranda ran down the stairs. 'What woman?'

'I don't know. I've never seen her before.'

'What did she look like?'

Holly closed her eyes, and tried to recall the stranger. 'She was in her thirties, I should think. Short dark hair. A very hard sort of face. She was wearing a short jacket and jeans.'

Miranda frowned. 'That doesn't sound like anyone I've ever seen around here.'

They looked round at the sound of more feet on the stairs. Tracy and Belinda came down to join them in the hall and Holly explained her encounter to all of them.

'And she just ran?' said Tracy.

'She took one look at me and bolted,' Holly confirmed.

Belinda went to the front door. 'There's no sign of it having been forced,' she said.

'It wasn't,' said Holly. 'She got in with a key.' She looked at Miranda. 'Does Suzannah hand out door keys to people?'

'Of course not,' said Miranda. 'I've got one. And so has Gail, but . . .' Her voice trailed off. 'Is Gail back yet?' she asked.

'No,' said Holly. 'I'd have heard. I haven't slept at all. I would have heard anyone coming in.'

'This is weird,' said Belinda. 'Do you think we should call the police?'

Holly switched the hall light on. 'I think so,' she said.

The four girls froze as they heard a step in the porch.

'She's back!' hissed Belinda. 'Quick! Put the chain on.'

Miranda ran forwards. The front door opened.

'What's all this?' asked a very surprised-looking Suzannah Winter. 'Shouldn't you girls be in bed at this hour?' She looked at their anxious faces. 'What's happened?' she asked.

In a confused babble of voices, they told her everything that had happened that evening, from the return and disappearance of Gail, to the midnight prowler.

'The only other person who had a key to this house was Gail,' said Suzannah. 'She's the only one who could have given a key to this woman that Holly saw.'

'But I'm sure I saw Gail get into the police car,' said Belinda.

'Except that she didn't tell *us* she was with the police,' said Holly. 'In fact, she seemed shocked that the police were after her. She said she was going straight to the police station to sort it out.'

'She certainly never turned up at the theatre,' said Suzannah. She reached for the telephone. 'I'm going to find out what's going on here.' She took a phone directory and found the number of the local police station.

The four girls stood silently in the hall during the conversation that Suzannah had on the phone.

From what they heard, it didn't seem to clarify things at all.

Suzannah put the receiver down. 'I can't make head nor tail of this,' she said to them. 'The police don't seem to know anything about Gail. They say no one from the local station was sent to call here for her, and Gail definitely hasn't been seen there this evening.'

'So who were the police officers that came here this afternoon?' asked Miranda.

'I've been given another number to ring in the morning,' said Suzannah. 'The phone number of the Narcotics Squad. The man I spoke to seemed to think they might know more about it.' Suzannah walked to the front door and put the chain on. 'Whatever Gail's up to, I don't want her back in this house until I've had a full explanation,' she said. 'Even if this drugs thing turns out to be nothing, I'll want to know how that woman got her hands on a front door key of mine.' She shook her head. 'I don't know,' she said. 'You do a person a favour, and the next thing you know your whole life is in chaos.'

There was nothing else to be done that night. Suzannah sent the girls off to bed and Holly tried again to make herself comfortable on the couch.

Despite the excitement, and despite having one ear open for the sound of Gail's return, Holly did eventually manage to drop off to sleep.

She felt that it was going to be a very interesting morning.

Charlotte made sure everyone was up and about early the next morning. The five of them were sitting on the floor in the sitting-room playing pick-up-sticks when Suzannah came down.

Gail had still not returned.

They had a quick breakfast of toast and coffee, then the four girls said goodbye to Charlotte and went back to Miranda's house.

They felt uncomfortable after the night at Suzannah's house, and they all had showers and a change of clothes before stretching themselves out in Miranda's garden and thinking about what they were going to do with the day.

'I hope we find out what all that business was about,' said Holly. 'It drives me mad having an unsolved mystery hanging over me.'

'It's not hanging over you,' said Belinda. 'It's hanging over Suzannah Winter. It's nothing to do with us.'

'Where's your curiosity?' Holly said, exasperated.

'I left it at home,' said Belinda. 'And I wish you had, too. Are we going sightseeing today, or what?'

A ring at the doorbell sent Miranda scuttling indoors.

It was Peter.

'It serves you right for avoiding baby-sitting,' Miranda said to him, after they had told him of their adventures.

'It sounds just like the old days,' said Peter. 'Holly, Miranda and I used to get tangled up in all sorts of peculiar things. Remember, Holly?'

'Yes,' said Holly. 'I remember.'

'Don't get her reminiscing,' said Tracy. 'We want to go do things, not sit here gabbing all day.'

'Did you know there was a funfair on Hampstead Heath?' said Peter. 'It arrived on Saturday and it's going to be there all week. I thought we could go and have a look.'

'A funfair?' said Belinda. 'If you lot think I'm going on any stomach-turning rides you can think again.'

'We could take Charlotte,' said Miranda. 'She'd *love* it.' She grinned at Belinda. 'You'd like to see her again, wouldn't you?'

'I wouldn't mind,' said Belinda. 'Charlotte and I could go on the kiddies' rides. That would be about exciting enough for me.' She smiled. 'And there'll be hot-dog stalls, won't there?'

'And cotton candy,' said Tracy. 'Sorry, you call it candy floss, don't you? Yes, let's do that. Go on, Miranda, give Suzannah a ring and tell her we'll take Charlotte out for the afternoon. It'll be great.'

There was no answer from Suzannah's house. But then Miranda remembered that there was a matinee performance of *The Snow Queen* that afternoon.

'Suzannah takes Charlotte to the theatre with her when there are afternoon performances,' explained Miranda. 'The backstage people look after her while Suzannah's on-stage. I don't think the performance starts until about three o'clock. We could go over to the theatre and ask Suzannah if it's OK to take Charlotte to the fair.'

'And at the same time,' Holly added, her eyes gleaming, 'we could ask her about Gail. I'm dying to know what's going on with her.'

The theatre was a grand old Victorian building. It dominated a corner of a long main street, its front brightened by a huge, colourful hoarding with a painting of Suzannah dressed as the Snow Queen in her ice palace.

Miranda took her four friends down the steeply sloping side street to the stage door. The small black door led into a narrow hallway with more doors and a staircase leading off. She told them she had been there a couple of times before, and that the doorman would know her.

Miranda rapped on a closed shutter. 'Hello? Anyone home?' she called.

The shutter opened to reveal an elderly man in a tiny room.

'Hello, Ted,' said Miranda. 'Can we see Suzannah at all?'

'She's in her dressing-room,' said Ted, eyeing the five of them. 'What's this? A visit from her fan club?'

'Just some friends,' said Miranda. 'Is Charlotte here?'

Ted grinned. 'She certainly is,' he said. 'Causing mischief as usual, I expect. But I'm not sure I should let you all in. We've got a show in forty minutes. I don't think the director will be very pleased to see armies of strangers wandering around backstage.'

'Oh, come on, Ted,' Miranda said persuasively. 'We'll only be five minutes. Suzannah knows us all.'

'Go on, then,' said Ted. 'But keep out of everyone's way.'

Miranda led her friends through some double doors and along a twisting corridor.

'It's not very glamorous, is it?' said Tracy, looking at the peeling paintwork and the grubby flooring.

'Backstage never is,' said Miranda. 'All the glamour is saved for the stage.'

'Do you think Suzannah will let us have a look round?' asked Peter. 'I've never been backstage in a real theatre before.'

They passed a number of doors and made a few turns before Miranda stopped in front of a door and knocked. Taped on to the door was a small label with Suzannah Winter's name printed on it.

They heard a call from within and Miranda opened the door.

It was a small white room with a few chairs in it and a large dressing-table with a mirror surrounded by bright lights. Suzannah was sitting at the mirror, carefully applying the white make-up that would transform her into the Snow Queen. Lying over the back of another chair was her ice-blue costume. It looked as if it was made of icicles sewn together.

At Suzannah's feet was a large, open case filled with theatrical make-up.

'Sorry to disturb you,' said Miranda. 'But we thought Charlotte might like to go to the fair on the Heath.'

Suzannah looked round at them, her face half white and half normal-coloured. 'I'm sure she would,' she said. 'If you don't mind taking her.'

'We'd love to,' said Holly.

Suzannah smiled, looking at Belinda. 'She'll be pleased to see you, in particular,' she said. 'She hasn't stopped talking about you all day. Apparently you're the best story-teller in the whole world.'

Belinda grinned. 'Perhaps I should become an actress,' she said. 'What are the hours like?'

'Long and hard,' said Suzannah with a laugh.

'Oh,' said Belinda. 'I'll just stick to telling brilliant bedtime stories, then. Where *is* Charlotte?'

'She's with Mary,' said Suzannah. 'Miranda, you know the way, don't you? They're up in the wings. I think Mary's showing her how the special effects work.'

'We'll find her,' said Miranda.

'By the way,' added Holly, 'have you seen anything of Gail?'

Suzannah's face darkened. 'No,' she said. 'No one has. She seems to have vanished completely. And I couldn't get any sense out of the police when I phoned them this morning either. I don't know where those police officers came from, but no one I've spoken to knows anything about them. I must say, I'm becoming very suspicious of Gail.' She shook her head. 'Her things are still at my house, but she's not going to be able to get them without speaking to me first. I've had the lock changed on the front door.'

'It's all very strange, isn't it?' said Tracy.

'I don't know about strange,' said Suzannah. 'It's extremely annoying. I've got a feeling we're not going to be seeing that Gail again. I think she's vanished on purpose.' She turned to the mirror and continued applying her make-up. 'I hope we shan't anyway,' she said. 'I'm too busy for all this nonsense. And it's the last time I'm going to let a complete stranger into my house, I can tell you that.'

Miranda took the friends along another corridor and up a narrow stairway. A few people in costume were running about, and other people seemed very busy with pieces of scenery and so on.

'We're in the wings,' said Miranda. 'Look. We'll have to keep very quiet.'

'You're telling *us* to be quiet?' said Belinda. 'You're the noisiest person I've ever met.'

'Have you seen the show?' asked Holly.

'Peter and I have watched a rehearsal,' said Miranda. 'But we haven't seen the whole thing.'

'It looked amazing in the rehearsals,' added Peter.

They craned for a glimpse of the stage. It was all dazzling blues and silvers with huge icy stalactites and stalagmites and a sparkling throne mid-stage on a raised platform.

'It's the Snow Queen's palace,' said Miranda. They could hear the orchestra tuning up, but in the gloom beyond the footlights the auditorium was empty.

They found Charlotte in a screened off corner with a woman and a couple of men. A large console stood in a glass booth against the wall, covered in dials and buttons and levers.

Charlotte seemed delighted to see them.

'I know all about the special effects now,' she said, grabbing Belinda. 'Look,' she said. 'If you pull this lever lots and lots of smoke goes all over the stage.'

'Dry ice,' explained Mary with a smile. 'It's not really smoke, but it gives a good impression. We can do everything from here. Snow. Rain. Thunder and lightning. And this dial makes the entire centre of the stage revolve. It's all controlled from here.'

The five friends watched in fascination as she showed them the workings of the console.

'I'd like a job doing something like that,' said Belinda. 'It looks like a lot of fun.'

'It's very skilled work,' said one of the men. 'The entire performance would collapse if we didn't know exactly what we were doing.'

Miranda crouched by Charlotte. 'Would you like to come to a funfair with us?' she asked.

Charlotte's eyes lit up. 'Yes, please,' she said, hugging her doll against herself. She put Polly's face to her ear and listened. 'Yes,' she said. 'Polly wants to go too. She says she's never been to a funfair before.'

'You'd better be off now,' said Mary. 'We've got to do all the last-minute preparations for the performance.'

'Come on, then,' said Peter. 'Off to the funfair. Last one on the Big Wheel is a wet fish!'

'I don't care,' said Belinda. 'You can call me a wet fish until the cows come home. You're not getting me up on that thing.'

They had been at the fair for an hour or more. Tracy had won a cuddly rabbit at a stall where you had to throw hoops over things. Holly had lost more ten pence pieces than she cared to count in a machine with sliding shelves full of coins that were always threatening to fall off, but never quite did.

They had indulged in a frantic, madcap ride on the dodgems, with Miranda's laugh echoing in their ears like a police siren. And her laughter had changed to piercing shrieks as things brushed over her and jumped out at her on the Ghost Train.

Peter had shot metal ducks with an air rifle and Belinda had failed miserably at the coconut shy.

They had been on chair rides which whirled them around until Belinda began to regret her third chunk of nougat.

But now they were standing under the Big Wheel, and Belinda was absolutely adamant that she wouldn't go on it.

'It's too high,' she explained. 'I hate heights. I wouldn't enjoy it at all. You lot go up, if you want to. I'll just watch from down here.'

'Polly and I will stay with Belinda,' said Charlotte, who had been holding Belinda's hand most of the afternoon. 'Polly says she doesn't like heights either.'

'There you are,' said Belinda. 'You lot go and make yourselves sick if you want to. Charlotte and I will have a nice, secure view of it all from down here.'

'I don't know how anyone can be such a coward,' said Tracy, as she and the others joined the queue for the Big Wheel.

'It's easy,' said Belinda. 'Anyone can be a coward if they practise at it enough.'

Belinda and Charlotte stood outside the wooden barrier and watched as the Big Wheel stopped and started to let people off and on.

They waved as Miranda and Peter were clamped into their chair and it went swinging into the air.

Holly waved down at them as the wheel spun another arc and she and Tracy were lifted, rocking, into the sky.

The wheel filled and began its giddy spin, the sound of laughter and shrieks echoing down, almost drowning out the clanging fairground music from the other rides.

'May I have a balloon?' asked Charlotte.

'Yes,' said Belinda. 'In a minute.'

Belinda waved every time her friends swept past, but it made her head spin just to think of what it must be like to be lifted up to that terrible height and sent plummeting earthwards.

'They're all completely mad, you know,' said Belinda, looking down to where Charlotte had been standing a moment before.

Charlotte was not there.

Belinda looked around, expecting at any moment to catch sight of the little girl in her bright blue dress.

'Charlotte!' called Belinda, her voice drowned by the loud pop music that clashed all around her. 'Charlotte!'

She ran this way and that, pushing past the crowds of people milling around the rides.

A rising panic filled her as she ran amongst the stalls, praying for a sight of Charlotte in all the confusion.

Where could she have gone?

Where could Charlotte possibly have gone?

5   A strange encounter

Don't panic. Don't panic, Belinda said to herself. *Charlotte can't have gone far. She's not silly.*

The noise of the fairground rides whirled and clattered in Belinda's ears as she bumped her way through the crowds in search of the little girl.

She can't be far away, Belinda thought. *There wasn't time. I only took my eyes off her for a second or two.*

But there were so many people, and so many rides and side-stalls. Charlotte could be just a few metres away and still be out of sight. She could be round the back of one of the stalls, or on the far side of the merry-go-round, completely unaware of the panic she was causing.

Belinda pushed her way back to the Big Wheel, desperately hoping that Charlotte might have gone back there.

Charlotte was nowhere to be seen, but at least the ride was coming to an end. Peter and Miranda came laughing down the wooden steps.

Their laughter faded as they saw Belinda's anguished face. A few seconds later Tracy and Holly had joined them.

'Did she say anything?' asked Miranda after Belinda had told them what had happened. 'Was there something that caught her eye?'

'I don't know,' said Belinda. She tried to think. She had been standing watching the Big Wheel spin. Charlotte had been at her side. Chattering. Chattering about what?

'Balloons!' gasped Belinda. 'She was saying something about balloons. About wanting a balloon.'

'Right,' said Peter. 'I've seen four or five people selling balloons. We should split up.'

'Whoever finds Charlotte brings her back here, OK?' said Tracy. She and Holly dived off into the crowds.

'I'll go this way,' said Peter, pointing in another direction. 'Don't worry,' he called back. 'We'll find her.'

'This is all my fault,' Belinda said miserably to Miranda. 'I couldn't even keep my eye on her for two minutes. What's Suzannah going to say?'

'Suzannah's not going to say anything,' Miranda said determinedly. 'Because we're going to find Charlotte. Come on. Come with me. We'll head over this way.'

'What if we *don't* find her?' said Belinda, pushing along in Miranda's wake.

'Don't even *think* about that,' Miranda said. She pointed ahead. Above the moving heads of the crowd a bright bunch of silvery balloons bobbed in the breeze. Balloons in the shape of rabbits and fish and parrots. Heart-shaped balloons, and huge yellow balloons like giant bananas.

The balloon-seller was sitting on an upturned crate, the balloons tied to a belt round his waist.

'Have you seen a little girl?' Miranda asked him, holding her hand out flat in front of her. 'About this height, with dark hair and a blue dress. Carrying a doll.'

The man shook his head. 'I've seen hundreds of little girls,' he said. 'If you've lost someone, your best bet is to go to the manager's caravan. It's over on the far side, behind the Big Wheel.'

'Yes. OK. Thanks.' Miranda grabbed Belinda's arm. 'He's right,' she said. 'They'll probably be able to put an announcement over the tannoy or something. Come on. Let's get over there.' She saw the anxiety in Belinda's face. 'Don't worry,' she said. 'I'll bet you anything you like one of the others has found her already.'

'I hope so,' said Belinda as they shoved their way back. 'I really hope so.'

Tracy and Holly had wound their way through the small side-stalls, making their way right across to the ring of caravans and engines that surrounded the fairground.

'We'll *never* find her,' said Tracy. 'For heaven's sake, how lost can one girl get?'

'Look!' Holly gave a gasp of relief. 'Look. There!'

She pointed down between two side-shows. A yellow balloon bobbed, and clinging to the string of the balloon was the familiar shape of a small girl with dark hair and a blue dress.

They pushed their way forwards and ran between the stalls.

'Charlotte!'

The little girl looked round. A man was crouched in front of her.

Charlotte waved and called to them. Her smile faded as she saw the expressions on their faces.

'Charlotte, you frightened the lives out of us,' gasped Holly. 'You mustn't run off like that. We thought we'd lost you.'

'I wanted a balloon,' said Charlotte. 'I wasn't lost.'

Holly knelt down and put her arms round Charlotte. 'You shouldn't have gone off like that,' she said, giving the little girl a fierce, relieved hug. 'It's not *safe*.'

The man stood up. 'She was OK,' he said. 'I saw she was on her own. I was just asking her who she belonged to.'

'He wanted to take Polly,' said Charlotte.

Tracy and Holly looked at the man, noticing that he had a doll under his arm. The man smiled and shrugged.

'I won this at the coconut shy,' he explained. 'I thought Lottie might like a new dolly instead of her old one.' He smiled down at Charlotte, holding the doll out. 'It's a much nicer dolly,' he said. 'Look at her lovely clean frock. And look how shiny her hair is. She's much nicer than your one, isn't she?'

'No,' said Charlotte, holding Polly tightly against herself. 'She's not nicer at all.'

'She wouldn't give Polly up for anything,' said Tracy. 'But thanks for trying to help.'

'We'd better find the others,' said Holly. She took a firm hold of Charlotte's hand.

The man moved round, still smiling and holding the doll out.

'Are you sure you wouldn't prefer a pretty new dolly?' he said to Charlotte. Holly couldn't be certain, but she thought she caught a glimpse of something odd in the man's face. It was as if his smile didn't quite reach his eyes.

'She doesn't want to swap,' said Holly. 'We'll take her back now. Our friends will be worrying.'

For a split second, as she moved forward, Holly got the impression that the man wasn't going to let them pass. But then he shrugged and stepped aside.

'Kids!' he said with a brief laugh.

As they headed towards the Big Wheel with Charlotte tucked safely between them, Tracy glanced round and saw the man staring stony-faced after them. Only for an instant. As he saw Tracy looking at him, he turned and melted into the crowds.

'Weird guy,' said Tracy. 'What was all that business with the doll?' She looked down at

Charlotte. 'How did you come to meet him, Charlotte?'

'I don't know,' said Charlotte. 'I was getting my balloon. He just followed me. I don't like him. He said nasty things about Polly.' She frowned up at the two girls. 'And he called me Lottie. I'm not Lottie. I'm *Charlotte*.' She hugged Polly. 'I don't like being called Lottie.'

'Don't worry,' said Holly. 'He's gone now. No one's going to take Polly away from you.'

'And we'll make sure no one calls you Lottie,' said Tracy with a smile. 'It's annoying, isn't it, when you tell someone your name and they go and shorten it like that?'

'I didn't,' said Charlotte.

Holly looked down at her. 'You didn't what?'

'I didn't – oh, look!' Charlotte let out a happy cry. 'Belinda!' She let go of Holly's hand and ran to Belinda.

'Charlotte!' yelled Belinda, clasping the little girl in her arms and spinning her round. 'You little monster! You frightened me to death! Where have you *been*?'

Miranda gave the other girls a look of relief.

'It's very naughty to go off like that on your own,' Miranda told Charlotte. 'What would your mummy have said if we'd come back without you?'

'I was getting a balloon,' said Charlotte, sliding down out of Belinda's arms. 'Are you cross with me?'

'No, of course not,' said Miranda. 'We were worried.'

'We'd better find Peter,' said Tracy. 'You guys stay here. I'll go look for him.'

They sat on the steps of the merry-go-round to wait for Tracy's return.

'We're going to have to put a lead on you,' Belinda said to Charlotte, tying the yellow balloon to Charlotte's wrist. 'Like dogs have. One of those extending leads so we can reel you in when you wander off.' Charlotte was sitting in Belinda's lap, her head on her shoulder.

'She's tired,' whispered Miranda, looking into Charlotte's sleepy face.

'I'm not,' murmured Charlotte. 'I'm not sleepy at all.'

'No,' said Miranda with a grin. 'I can see that.' She mouthed quietly to Holly, 'She'll be out like a light in a few minutes. I think we'd better take her home.'

'Not . . . sleepy . . .' mumbled Charlotte, settling herself comfortably against Belinda.

By the time Tracy arrived back with Peter, Charlotte was almost asleep.

'Can you carry her to the bus stop?' asked Miranda. 'It's not far.'

'I think so,' said Belinda.

'Oh, hang on,' said Miranda. 'I've just remembered. Suzannah's had the lock changed on her front door, hasn't she? We won't be able to get in.'

'We could go back to your place,' said Holly. 'She could have a sleep there. We'll take her back to Suzannah's later on.'

Belinda heaved herself to her feet, her hands clasped under Charlotte, the sleeping girl's head lolling on her shoulder.

'Crumbs,' said Belinda. 'She weighs a ton. Come on, let's get her home before my arms drop off.'

'She doesn't usually crash out in the afternoon,' whispered Miranda, tucking a blanket round Charlotte and creeping away from the sofa where Belinda had laid her.

'It must have been all the excitement of the fairground,' said Holly with a grin. 'She'll probably be racing around like a mad thing all evening once she wakes up.'

'Let's go through into the kitchen so we don't disturb her,' said Miranda. 'We can plan tomorrow's outings.'

'What about the rest of *today's* outings?' said Peter. 'It's only half past five. There's plenty we can still do. Where's that list I made?'

They sat at the kitchen table. Peter looked at his list. The four girls had scribbled their own ideas all over it, crossing things out and adding other things.

'It's a bit of a mess now, isn't it?' he said. 'Perhaps we'd better start again.'

'I picked up some leaflets,' said Miranda. 'Let's have a look through them.'

There seemed to be an enormous amount going on in London. Their biggest problem was trying to think of a way to fit in as much sightseeing as possible in the short time they had.

Peter soon recovered from having his carefully-planned agenda discarded, and they got out a big map of the city to help locate all the different places they wanted to visit. 'I'd really like to see *this*,' said Peter, picking out a black leaflet with a skull and crossbones on it. In gothic print were written the words 'The Crypt Under The Bridge'.

'A couple of friends of mine have already been there. They said it was brilliant,' he told them. 'It only opened a few weeks ago.'

'What's it all about?' asked Holly.

'Murders,' Peter said with relish. 'Murders and terrible crimes that have been committed in London over the past few hundred years. It's in a series of old cellars by the Thames. They've got a model torture chamber and an entire street down there set up to look just like the place where Jack the Ripper operated.'

'Delightful,' said Belinda. 'It sounds like good family entertainment. Who'd want to bother with Tower Bridge when they could spend the day in a dank cellar up to their ears in blood and gore?'

'We can't go there today,' said Miranda. 'It'll be

closed by now. And anyway, we can't go *anywhere* until we've dropped Charlotte off.'

'We could do it tomorrow afternoon,' said Peter. 'If we met up at Trafalgar Square in the morning, we could go on one of those bus tours first, and then see the Crypt in the afternoon. It's supposed to be dead scary.' He looked at Holly. 'You like that sort of thing, don't you?' he said. 'It tells you all about how these crimes were solved and everything.'

'I'm up for it,' said Tracy, reading the leaflet. 'It says they've got one of those chair rides as well. "Murders down the ages".' She read aloud from the leaflet. '"You will be taken on a ride through the darker side of Old London, experiencing the sights, sounds and smells of the grislier aspects of our past".' She grinned at the others. 'Let's go there, huh? It sounds like fun.'.

'OK,' Belinda said to Tracy. 'But I'll want a pair of earmuffs in case Miranda does one of her deafening screams down there. I've still got the ringing in my ears from the Ghost Train.'

'Anyone would think I was loud,' said Miranda.

'Loud?' said Belinda. 'It was like having an elephant trumpeting in your ear.'

'What about this evening?' said Peter. 'We could get a tube down to Covent Garden. There's always plenty going on there. Street performers and so on.'

'Good idea,' said Miranda. 'I'll see if my mum

will drop Charlotte off at home when she gets in, and we could go straight off from there.' She stood up. 'I've just had a thought,' she said. 'I won't be a minute. I'm just going to get your tickets for *The Snow Queen*,' she said. 'That way I won't be responsible if they get lost.'

She went up to her room and came back with the five tickets. 'I suppose you'll be able to take a night off from playing with that car of yours,' she said to Peter.

'We're not *playing* with it,' Peter said, affronted. 'We're customising it, for your information.' He looked at the ticket. It was dated for the day after tomorrow. Curtain up at seven-thirty. 'I've already told Keith and Simon I won't be able to help much more this week.'

'What are you actually doing with it?' asked Tracy.

Peter spent a few minutes explaining how they were stripping the car down ready to put a new supercharged engine in it. 'And we're going to paint flames down the sides,' he said. 'It'll look amazing. Keith reckons we'll be able to do two hundred and forty kilometres an hour in it.'

'Isn't that a bit above the speed limit?' asked Belinda.

'That's not the point,' said Peter.

'Don't get him talking about it,' said Miranda. 'We'll be here all night if you do.'

Peter frowned at her. 'You just don't understand about cars,' he said. He looked at Belinda. 'You see, the whole point of customising a car is— '

'Here's my mum,' interrupted Miranda, hearing a sound from the hall. She laughed. 'In the nick of time, too.'

She went to speak to her mother, the others following her out into the hall.

Mrs Hunt glanced into the sitting-room as they told her about their afternoon with Charlotte at the fair.

'Give Suzannah a ring, to make sure she's home,' said Mrs Hunt. 'Then I'll drive you over there.' She looked at the others. 'And while I'm doing that, the rest of you could be getting dinner ready.'

'That's a good idea,' said Belinda. 'I haven't eaten all day.'

Tracy stared at her. 'What about the hot-dog?' she said. 'And that bar of nougat? And the pea-nuts.'

'They don't count,' said Belinda airily. 'I was talking about proper eating. Those were snacks.'

Miranda and her mother had taken the still half-asleep Charlotte off in the car, and Holly was folding up the blanket the little girl had been sleeping under when she noticed the lop-sided smiling face of Charlotte's doll on the sofa.

'She's forgotten Polly,' said Holly, picking the limp doll up.

Tracy looked over her shoulder. 'She could do with half an hour in a washing machine,' she said. 'Look at the state of her hair.'

'She's not dirty,' said Holly. 'Just old. Her dress is all coming to pieces as well.' Holly turned the doll over on to its face, trying to pull the crumpled dress straight. 'Look,' she said, lifting the dress. 'She's coming unstitched all down the back. The stuffing's going to come out if that isn't mended.'

'Don't look at me,' said Belinda. 'I couldn't sew a straight line to save my life.'

'I'll get some thread from Miranda later,' said Holly. 'We can't do much about the rest of her, but at least I can sew the seam up.' She put the doll down on the sofa and the three of them went off into the kitchen to start preparing dinner.

Later that evening the four girls were back in Miranda's bedroom, discussing their outing. They had spent a couple of hours in Covent Garden, looking around the shops and sitting on the pavement watching the street performers.

There had been a quartet of Chinese musicians in the covered area. Outside, other people had banged an assortment of drums while a man balanced bottles and chairs on his chin. But the most exciting part had been a fire-eater who blew great gouts of flame from his mouth.

70

The place had still been crowded even when they had left.

They had arranged to meet Peter at Trafalgar Square at ten o'clock the following morning for their bus tour.

'This room certainly suits your personality,' said Belinda, looking at the bright yellow walls and the huge colourful posters of film stars. There was a cork notice-board above her bed, covered in postcards and photographs.

'Look at this,' Tracy said, spotting an old photo. 'It's Holly! How old were you then? Look how thin you were.'

'I was twelve,' Holly said, as Miranda pointed out to Tracy and Belinda other photos that included Holly and Peter.

When they had finished reminiscing and laughing over the old photographs, Holly sat cross-legged on Miranda's bed and set about mending the gaping back seam of Charlotte's doll with a needle and thread.

'You're so domesticated,' said Belinda with a laugh, sprawling lazily on the carpet. 'You'll make someone a wonderful little wife one day.'

Holly broke off from her work to poke her tongue out at Belinda.

'Charlotte's going to be real upset when she wakes up and finds Polly is missing,' said Tracy. 'It was bad enough that guy trying to make her do that swap at the fairground.'

71

'What swap?' asked Miranda.

'Oh, we forgot to tell you,' said Tracy. She explained about the strange man at the fairground.

'And she wasn't very pleased with him calling her Lottie, either,' added Holly.

Miranda sat up. 'He called her Lottie? Are you sure?'

'Positive,' said Tracy. She looked across at Holly. 'What was it she said, Holly?'

Holly was frowning, the needle poised in mid-air. 'I've just remembered something,' she said. She looked at Tracy. 'When we were coming back to find the others, you said something about it being annoying when people shorten your name after you've told it to them. And Charlotte said "I didn't". Remember?'

'Kind of,' said Tracy. 'It was just before we met up with Belinda and Miranda.'

'That's right,' said Holly. 'I've only just remembered. Charlotte said "I didn't".' She looked at the others. 'Do you think she meant she hadn't told him her name?'

'She must have done,' said Belinda. 'How would he have known to call her Lottie otherwise?'

'She wouldn't have said she was called Lottie,' said Miranda. 'She'd have said Charlotte.'

'Yes, but— ' began Belinda.

'The only person who calls her Lottie is Gail,' said Miranda, her eyes widening.

'Hang on,' said Tracy. 'This doesn't make any

sense. What are you saying? That this guy at the fairground was something to do with Gail? He can't have been. It's got to be some kind of weird coincidence.'

Belinda lifted herself from her sprawl on the floor. 'What did the man look like?' she asked eagerly. 'Can you describe him?'

'He was in his late thirties, I should think,' said Holly. 'Not very tall. Quite stockily built. With dark hair.'

'And he had a brown leather jacket,' added Tracy. 'I remember that.'

Belinda sat with her hands over her mouth. 'I don't want to worry you,' she said slowly. 'I mean, I could be wrong.'

'Wrong about what?' asked Holly.

'Well,' breathed Belinda, gazing round at her friends. 'That description you've just given fits the man I saw Gail talking to last night. The man in the car. The car that the police were in yesterday at Suzannah's house. The man she drove off with when she said she was going to the police station.' She paused for a moment, as her three friends stared silently at her.

She blinked at them and nodded. 'It sounds like him,' she said breathlessly. 'It sounds like it was the same man.'

6 Thief!

Holly ran up the stairs to the top of the house and hammered on Tracy and Belinda's bedroom door.

'Time to get up!' she yelled.

'It's OK,' Tracy shouted from within. 'I'm awake.'

'Breakfast is ready,' called Holly, running back down. 'It's on the table.'

Tracy pulled the curtains and opened the window. She looked out over the garden and the houses of North London, marching away into the distance, punctuated by trees and church spires. It was so different from the view that met her eyes every morning in Willow Dale, where the small town seemed to be cupped in the sheltering hand of the Yorkshire hills.

There was a groan from the unmade bed, and a lump moved to pull blankets over its head.

'Come on, you sloth,' said Tracy, running over to Belinda's bed and giving her a shake.

'Five more minutes,' mumbled Belinda.

'Breakfast is ready,' said Tracy, going over to the window again and brushing her hair in the bright sunlight.

Belinda muttered something and heaved her pillow up over her head.

'Good heavens,' said Tracy. 'You wouldn't think these gardens were big enough for people to keep a horse in.'

Belinda sat up. 'What did you say?'

'The garden next door,' said Tracy, leaning out of the window. 'There isn't room for a stable, surely?'

Belinda scrambled down her bed and peered short-sightedly out of the window. 'Where?'

'Where what?' asked Tracy.

'The horse,' said Belinda. 'You said something about a horse next door.'

'No,' said Tracy with a grin. 'I said surely these gardens *aren't* big enough to keep a horse in. And they aren't.' She laughed. 'It got you out of bed, though, didn't it?'

'You rat!' said Belinda, realising she had been fooled.

Tracy went to the door. 'Breakfast is on the table,' she said.

She had a wash, then went down to the kitchen just as Miranda was taking croissants out of the oven.

Polly the doll was sitting on the table.

'Poor Charlotte,' said Tracy, looking at the doll. 'She must be wondering where Polly's gotten to.'

'It's OK,' said Holly, pouring out orange juice. 'Miranda and I are going to pop over to Suzannah's place on the way to Trafalgar Square. We'll drop Polly off and meet up with you and Peter a bit later.'

A few minutes later Belinda arrived, and the four of them sat down to breakfast.

By half past nine they had cleared up and were ready to leave. Holly and Miranda headed for the bus stop to go to Suzannah's house, while Belinda and Tracy set off for the tube station.

Miranda's instructions for getting to Trafalgar Square were simple. A single Underground train would take them all the way there. Once at Charing Cross station they should head for the Trafalgar Square exit, and they'd see the National Gallery on the far side of the square. They'd agreed to meet on the steps of the museum.

A train was pulling in as they came on to the platform and they ran to get on board before the doors hissed closed.

'Are you sure about this?' Belinda asked Tracy, as they sat down. 'Are we on the right train?'

'Sure,' said Tracy. 'Miranda said eleven stops and we'd be there.'

'You're certain?' said Belinda dubiously.

'Absolutely,'said Tracy.

A quarter of an hour later, and Belinda was even less convinced than before.

'I don't remember Miranda mentioning any of the stops, we've been through,' said Belinda. 'We're on the wrong train.'

'How can we be?' said Tracy. 'Don't make such a fuss, Belinda. I know what I'm doing.'

Belinda looked uneasily at her. 'That's what worries me,' she said.

Holly and Miranda walked up the path to Suzannah Winter's house. Holly was carrying Polly in a white plastic bag.

Miranda rang the bell and they waited.

She rang again, but still no one came to the door.

'They must be out,' said Holly.

'Looks like it,' said Miranda. 'And my key doesn't fit the lock now Suzannah's had it changed.' She went to the window and peered through. She shook her head.

'No,' she said. 'No sign of life.'

Holly took Polly out of the bag. 'Shall we just leave her on the doorstep?' she said.

'I don't think so,' said Miranda. 'She might get stolen. Charlotte would have a fit. We'd better take her with us and give her back later.'

As she came back to the path, she noticed that Holly's eyes were fixed on something further down the road. Miranda followed the line of Holly's gaze. The kerbs on both sides of the road were filled with parked cars.

'What are you looking at?' she asked Holly.

'I'm not sure,' said Holly. 'That blue car. Right down the end there. Isn't that the same car that the police were in the other day?'

'I don't know,' said Miranda, shielding her eyes from the sunlight. 'It's similar all right. It's a pity Peter isn't here. He'd be able to tell you if it was the same one or not.'

'There's someone sitting in it,' said Holly. 'I'm sure there is.'

'It can't be the same one,' said Miranda. 'There must be hundreds of cars like that around here.'

'I'm going to have a closer look,' said Holly.

As she walked down the path the car drove slowly away round the curve of the crescent and disappeared.

'See?' said Miranda. 'It wasn't the same one.'

'I think it was,' said Holly. 'Whoever was in it saw me coming.' She looked meaningfully at Miranda. 'I think they're watching the house.'

'I suppose they *could* be,' said Miranda. 'It would make sense, wouldn't it, if they're out to arrest Gail. They'd expect her to come back here at some stage, wouldn't they?'

'If it *is* the police at all,' said Holly. 'Remember that Suzannah said she couldn't get through to anyone at the police station who knew anything about Gail. I wonder.'

'It's probably a secret undercover operation,' said Miranda. 'That's why they wouldn't tell Suzannah what was going on.'

Holly shook her head. 'They came here in uniform,' she said. 'They wouldn't have done that if it was an undercover operation. I think there's more to it than that.'

'Look,' said Miranda. 'We haven't got time to worry about this now.' She looked at her watch. 'We're late for meeting Peter as it is. We can always tell Suzannah about it next time we see her.'

Holly put the doll back into the bag. 'OK,' she said. 'Let's go, then.'

They took a bus back to Highgate Underground station and got on to a southbound train to take them down to Charing Cross.

The train filled rapidly as they headed into the centre of London, and by the time they had reached Charing Cross the passengers were packed like sardines in the aisles.

'I'd almost forgotten how full these trains get,' shouted Holly above the noise of the train as they fought their way through the scrum of people to get to the opening doors.

There was a lot of chaos in the doorway as people getting off tangled up with the crowds trying to get on.

Miranda popped out on to the platform like a cork coming out of a bottle.

Holly was in the middle of the crush. As she pushed forwards she felt something catch hold of the white plastic bag and wrench it away from her. She tried to turn, to shoulder her way back on to the train, but the press of people shoved her out on to the platform.

'The bag!' gasped Holly. 'Someone's stolen the bag. Someone pulled it out of my hand in there.'

'Quick!' said Miranda. 'Get back on.'

A wall of bodies blocked the doorway. The train was packed solid. Holly managed to get her shoulder between two people and wedge her way forwards.

Miranda was right behind her, but before she could get her foot up on to the train she heard the hiss of the doors beginning to close.

'Holly!' Aggressive faces stared at her as she tried to force her way on to the jammed train. 'Holly, I can't—'

The doors thudded closed. Miranda saw a brief glimpse of Holly's hair as the train pulled away.

She stood staring as the carriages swept past and the train vanished noisily into the tunnel.

Holly was on her own.

'I told you we were on the wrong train,' said Belinda. 'But you knew best, as always.'

'It's not my fault,' said Tracy. 'How was I supposed to know there were two branches to the Northern Line? They should have signs up.'

'They *do*,' said Belinda. 'If you could be bothered to look.'

They were standing on the platform of the eleventh tube station. It should have been Charing Cross. It was actually London Bridge.

There was a large map of the entire Underground

system on the wall. Belinda's finger traced the route they should have taken. They had accidentally got on a train that looped round in an alternative route.

Tracy looked at her watch. It was after ten o'clock already. 'So now what do we do?' she asked. 'Go back to Highgate and start again?'

'No,' said Belinda. 'I've got it sussed. We go two stops further south, then change to the Bakerloo Line northbound. That'll take us straight to Charing Cross.'

'Are you sure?' said Tracy. 'We're going to be really late.'

'I'm sure,' said Belinda, sitting down.

Tracy sat down next to her. 'This sure is a complicated city,' she sighed.

Belinda laughed. 'It is when *you're* navigating,' she said.

Twenty minutes later Belinda led her up the steps of the exit of Charing Cross station and they saw Trafalgar Square in front of them.

The white square was teeming with people, sitting on the edges of the fountains, climbing over the huge black lions to have their photographs taken. Rising high and aloof into the brilliant blue sky, Nelson stood on his towering column, staring out over the traffic-filled streets.

The two girls crossed the road.

'That must be the National Gallery,' said Belinda, pointing to a massive building on the far side of the square. 'The others will all be there by now, wondering where we've got to. Thanks to your little diversion.'

Mobs of pigeons eddied around their feet as they made their way across the square.

'Yuck!' said Belinda as the grey birds scuttled to and fro across their path. 'Rats with wings. Filthy-looking things.'

'They can't help it,' said Tracy. 'I think they're kind of cute. Do we have time to buy some stuff to feed them?'

'No, we haven't,' Belinda said firmly.

They climbed the broad steps to join the crowds waiting to cross the road.

'Can you see Peter or anyone?' asked Tracy.

'No, I can't,' said Belinda. 'There are so many people around here. Oh! Hold on. Look!' She pointed. The entrance to the National Gallery lifted high above the streets, approached from either side by flights of stone steps. Standing by the railings that fronted the pillared entrance, Belinda could see Peter looking out.

The two girls ran up the steps.

'Sorry we're late,' panted Belinda. 'Tracy got us lost.'

'I did not,' said Tracy. 'It was that dumb train.' She looked around. 'Where are Holly and Miranda?'

'That's what I'd like to know,' said Peter. 'I thought we said ten o'clock. It's nearly half past.'

Belinda gave him a puzzled look. 'They should have been here ages ago,' she said.

'Perhaps *they* got lost as well,' said Tracy. 'It's easy enough to do.'

'Not if you *live* in London,' said Belinda. 'They must have got held up somewhere.' She explained to Peter about Miranda and Holly's plan to drop the doll off at Suzannah Winter's house.

'Even so,' said Peter. 'That shouldn't have delayed them for more than twenty minutes at most.' He looked at the two girls, and then down into the crowded square.

He frowned at them. 'So?' he said. 'Where are they?'

Holly could hardly move. The jam-packed bodies left her with just enough room to reach up and grab an overhead rail to stop herself being bounced around like a pinball.

She had seen Miranda's anxious face for a second as the doors had closed. And then the train had jerked away from the station and Holly had realised she was on her own.

She had lived all her life in London. She knew how thieves sometimes haunted crowded places, waiting for their chance to pick pockets and steal bags. But it had never happened to her before and she wasn't sure what she should do.

There was an emergency lever, but she didn't know what the effect would be of pulling it. It might just stop the train in the tunnel. She didn't fancy doing that. Tube trains were hot and claustrophobic

83

enough, without finding herself trapped between stations in this crush of people.

If only she could find the person who had taken her bag, she could alert a guard at the next station and have the thief picked up before he could get away.

She stretched on tiptoe, trying to see above the heads and shoulders that surrounded her. If only she could *move*.

A shock went through her. At the far end of the carriage she saw a woman's face for an instant. The woman looked away immediately, but in that second, Holly recognised the hard, sharp lines of the faces, and the dark, cold eyes. It was the woman she had encountered in Suzannah Winter's hall the other night. Holly was certain of it.

It wasn't a face she could easily forget, even at that distance and in those confusing conditions.

As the train rattled along, Holly saw the woman shoulder her way to the door at the far end of the carriage.

Light flickered through the train windows. They were coming to the next station. Holly looked at the signs. Embankment. This was the last station north of the River Thames. After this, the train would sweep away southwards, taking her into parts of London that she didn't know. The idea alarmed her.

Holly kept her eyes fixed on the back of the woman's head, waiting to see what she was going to do. Holly felt sure that it was this woman who had stolen her bag. It was too much of a coincidence.

The train slowed and came to a halt. The platform was less crowded than Charing Cross had been.

The doors hissed open and Holly was surrounded by movement as people fought to get off.

She lost sight of the woman.

Had she got off or not?

Then Holly saw her on the platform, walking quickly in the crowd, a white carrier bag crammed under her arm.

Holly jumped off the train, her eyes searching for someone in a uniform. Someone she could ask for help.

There didn't seem to be anyone.

Holly dodged through the crowds, trying to keep the woman in sight. She knew there would be a guard or someone at the ticket barrier. They would help her.

The woman glanced round and Holly felt the chilling touch of her eyes. The woman had seen her. She knew she was being followed.

There was a hiss as the train doors began to close. The woman made a sudden movement across the platform and stepped on to the train as the doors closed behind her.

'No, *you don't!*' thought Holly, making a leap towards the train, jamming her foot between the doors. The rubber edges of the doors squeezed against her as she fought to pull them open.

Someone from inside forced the doors wider for her and she eased into the gap.

'You nearly missed it,' said the man.

'Yes,' gasped Holly. 'Thanks.' The doors bumped together.

The woman was in the next carriage along. Holly walked along the aisle to be nearer to her.

Suddenly the doors opened again for the space of two heartbeats before thudding finally together. The train began to move.

Holly ran to the door, but it was too late. In that brief moment when the doors had opened again, the woman had jumped off the train.

Holly saw her walking along the platform towards the exit as the train swept her away.

There was no way of getting off the train now until the next station. And by the time she got there and found someone to report the incident to, Holly knew the woman would be long gone.

Holly gave the door a frustrated thump with her fist, staring at her own angry reflection in the glass panel.

Her only comfort was that, whatever the woman had thought Holly was carrying in the bag, she was going to be disappointed when she opened it and found only Charlotte's doll in there.

Holly frowned.

Unless, of course, it was the doll she was after.

But why? Why would anyone want to steal an old rag doll?

7 The Crypt Under The Bridge

Miranda stared after the departing tube train as it snaked away into the tunnel with Holly and the thief on board. The echoing noise faded into an eerie silence.

The few people left on the platform were heading for the exits. Miranda stood indecisively at the platform's edge, frowning as she looked into the dark mouth of the tunnel.

Now what do I do? she thought, biting her lip. *Wait for the next train? Follow Holly?* She looked up at the arrivals board. It promised another train in six minutes.

No. That would be no good. How was she to know which station Holly might get off at?

What would Holly do? thought Miranda. Would she follow the thief? In which case there was nothing Miranda could do to help. Or would she get off the train at the next station and catch the first train back?

Knowing Holly, she might well follow the person who had snatched her bag. That would be just like her.

Miranda went to the platform exit and crossed to the northbound platform.

I'll give it ten minutes, she thought. *If Holly's not on one of these trains in that time, I'll go up and tell someone what's happened.*

She watched the passengers getting off the first northbound train. Holly wasn't amongst them.

Two more trains stopped and let off passengers as Miranda waited with growing unease. There was no sign of Holly.

Miranda looked at her watch. The ten minutes were up. She headed for the escalator.

She was about to step on to the escalator when she heard the arrival of another train. She hesitated at the foot of the moving stairway, standing aside to allow the disembarked passengers to pass her.

She shook her head. Still Holly had not appeared. With a growing concern tightening in her stomach, Miranda stepped on to the escalator.

'Miranda!'

She looked down. Holly was there.

Miranda forced her way down the rising metal stairs.

'I couldn't get on the train,' Miranda gasped. 'I didn't know what to do. What happened?'

'I lost her,' said Holly.

'Her?'

Holly nodded. 'It was the woman from Suzannah's house. I saw her. She had my bag.'

'I don't get it,' said Miranda. 'If it *was* her, why should she steal a plastic bag from you?'

'I'm not sure yet,' said Holly. 'But I'm beginning to see some sort of pattern to all this. Look, let's get to the others. We need to talk.'

'Let's give them another five minutes,' said Peter.

'Then what?' asked Belinda. 'Send out search parties?'

'Where can they have gotten to?' said Tracy. 'You don't think something's happened to them?'

'Holly can look after herself,' said Belinda.

'So can Miranda,' said Peter. 'But they're nearly an hour late.'

'Maybe we should go look for them?' suggested Tracy.

'No,' said Belinda. 'We'd be chasing around like headless chickens. Our best bet is to stay here and wait. They'll turn up.'

They leaned over the iron rail, scanning the busy streets for any sign of their missing friends.

'There they are!' shouted Tracy. 'Look! Over there. Coming across the square.'

The three friends ran down the steps.

'They'd better have a really good excuse for this,' said Belinda. 'If they've been wandering around enjoying themselves I'll strangle them. I could have spent all this time quite happily in bed.'

Peter, Tracy and Belinda listened in amazement as Holly told them what had happened.

'That's crazy,' said Tracy. 'What was in the bag?'

'Only Charlotte's doll,' said Holly. She looked at her friends. 'I think we ought to go somewhere and think this through.'

'There's a place just across the road where we can get a drink,' said Peter. 'We can talk there.'

They grabbed a window table and sat drinking Coke as Holly explained her thoughts.

'I think it was the doll that she was after,' said Holly. 'It's the only way any of this makes any sense. There's got to be something about that doll.' She pulled the Mystery Club's notebook out of her shoulder bag. 'Let's write this down,' she said. 'Point by point. Everything that's happened since the police came to arrest Gail.'

They went slowly through all the incidents of the past couple of days.

'I'll tell you one thing,' said Miranda. 'I don't believe those people *were* from the police. Whatever Gail's involved in, I think they're part of it.'

'And that weird guy at the fairground is one of them,' said Tracy. 'He was trying to get the doll off Charlotte.'

'And I saw him with Gail when she was supposed to be going to the police station,' said Belinda. She put her hand to her mouth. 'Oh! And Gail came up to Charlotte's room that night. She said she wanted to say goodnight to her. I didn't think anything of it at the time, but she could have been hoping to get her hands on the doll then.'

'So what *is* it with the doll?' said Tracy.

'Drugs,' said Peter. 'Those people pretending to be from the police told Suzannah that it was something to do with drugs. Perhaps Gail hid the drugs in the doll?'

'I don't think so,' said Holly. 'The back of the doll was split open, remember? I sewed it up. If there had been anything like that in there I'd have seen it.'

'Wait a minute,' said Belinda. 'I still can't figure this out. If that man and woman are working *with* Gail, why should they go round to Suzannah's house pretending to be the police? It doesn't make any sense.'

'She's right,' said Miranda. 'None of this makes sense.'

'It does,' Holly said determinedly. 'It *must*. We just can't see it yet.'

'I'm going to phone Suzannah,' said Miranda. 'I think she ought to be told what's been happening.'

The other four waited while Miranda went to the phone. She came back a minute later.

'No answer,' she said. 'She must still be out. She could be out all day for all I know. What should we do now?'

'We could go back to Suzannah's house and have a look in Gail's room,' said Belinda. 'Remember,

Suzannah said all her stuff is still in there? We might find something.'

Miranda shook her head. 'We can't get in,' she said. 'My key doesn't fit the lock any more.'

'Listen,' said Peter. 'If we're right, and they *were* after the doll . . .' He looked round at them and shrugged. 'They've got it now, haven't they?'

'Yes,' said Holly. 'So?'

'So there's nothing we can do,' explained Peter. 'I think we should carry on today doing what we planned on doing, then go to Suzannah's house later this afternoon.' He looked at Miranda. 'She should be back by then, shouldn't she?'

'I don't know,' said Miranda. 'I suppose so.'

'Right,' said Peter. 'We'll go there later this afternoon and tell her what we've been talking about. Tell her about the doll and everything and leave her to get in touch with the police.'

'The *real* police,' added Belinda. 'I think Peter's right. If there are drugs at the bottom of this, I don't fancy us getting any more involved than we already are.' She blew her cheeks out. 'And this is supposed to be a *holiday*!' she said.

They talked things over for a while longer, finally agreeing on Peter's plan.

'So?' said Holly. 'Where do we go?'

'The tour buses pick people up on the hour from Trafalgar Square,' said Peter. 'The tours take about an hour and a half, so that'll give us plenty of time to visit the Crypt as well.'

Holly nodded and stood up. 'Come on then, let's see some sights,' she said.

'At last!' said Tracy.

They bought their tickets from a waiting courier and made their way up on to the open top of the double-decker bus.

'And on your left,' said Miranda, gesturing grandly, 'you cán see Admiral Lord Nelson standing on the pillar they erected to celebrate his victory at the Battle of Trafalgar.'

'I wonder what they'd have done if he'd lost,' said Belinda. 'Dug a hole?'

Miranda yelled with laughter.

A young woman came and stood at the front of the bus as they set off, giving them a running commentary as the bus wound its slow way through the fascinating streets of the city.

The tour took them past the ancient walls of the Tower of London, gleaming white in the sunlight. Tower Bridge rose majestically ahead of them, solid as a rock as it spanned the wide, brown waters of the Thames. Sunlight flared on the golden globe that topped the Monument erected to commemorate the Great Fire, and as the bus turned, the young woman pointed out the impressive face of the Bank of England. Then they went past St Paul's Cathedral and down along the Embankment to the Houses of Parliament and Westminster Abbey.

It seemed like only a few minutes before they

were back in Trafalgar Square and the tour was over.

'Now where?' asked Holly, as they gathered on the pavement.

'To the Crypt?' suggested Peter.

They made their way to the Underground station that would take them to The Crypt Under The Bridge.

It was one of a row of arched entrances in a high-walled street near the River Thames. A number of people were crowded round the entrance. Above the door a painted skull stared down at the five friends as they joined the queue to get in.

Holly was only half-convinced that they should be doing this rather than trying to find out about the missing doll. But she reconciled herself to the fact that Peter was probably right. There really wasn't anything they *could* do at the moment. And now that Gail and the other two had got the doll there didn't seem to be any immediate danger. So long as it really *was* the doll that they were after.

The puzzle of the past two days still rankled with Holly as they bought their tickets and went into the gloomy Crypt. They found themselves in a high-arched, dimly-lit hall.

'Oh, no,' said Tracy, looking up. 'Bats!'

'They're not real,' said Belinda, squinting up through her spectacles to the dark shapes that hung from the lofty roof.

Skeletons hung in chains on the walls, and creepy, gloomy music was playing in the background. The hallway branched out into a series of shadowy rooms.

'Isn't this great?' said Peter, staring through rusty iron bars into a small room bathed in blood-red light. A waxwork figure held an axe and another figure was bent over a red-spattered wooden block. There was a sudden rush of noise and movement as the axe fell and the waxworks head plopped into a waiting basket.

Miranda screamed, making everyone jump. She looked round, shamefaced, her hands over her mouth.

'Sorry,' she said. 'I wasn't expecting the head actually to come off.'

'You're worse than the exhibits,' said Belinda, wiggling her finger in her ear. 'I should have brought earplugs.'

Similar gory scenes were played out as the five friends wound their way through the grisly exhibits.

A man in a bushy moustache filled a bathtub with acid while his victim lay dead on the floor.

'They must get through a lot of tomato ketchup,' said Belinda, wincing as a knife rose and fell and an unearthly scream rang out. 'And to think we *paid* to be frightened half to death.'

Creaks and groans filled the air as some poor soul was stretched on a torture rack.

'It reminds me of the gym back at school,' Belinda said to Tracy. 'Mrs Bannister would probably love to get her hands on some of these things.'

'Look,' said Miranda. 'There's the entrance to the chair-ride.' They headed towards the low, arched tunnel where a group of people were waiting for their turn on the ride.

It was darker than ever in the tunnel as the hooded chairs moved slowly into sight and a guide ushered people on.

'It's just like the Ghost Train,' said Holly.

Peter grinned round at her. 'Except that everything we're going to see really happened,' he said.

'Thanks for reminding me,' said Belinda. 'Miranda? Can you try and control yourself in here, please?'

The solitary chairs glided silently on their rails as the five friends came to the front of the queue.

'Only four to a chair,' said the guide, as Peter climbed aboard.

'I'll get the next one,' said Holly. 'You four go on ahead.'

'See you at the other end,' said Tracy with a grin. 'With any luck.'

The loaded chair spun and slowly edged into darkness as the next chair slid into its place.

There was room for two people at the front and two at the back. Holly got into the front. She heard someone climb in behind her.

No one else got on board and the chair began

to move off. A recorded voice whispered from a concealed speaker somewhere in the chair's roof.

'Prepare yourself to be taken back through the centuries,' it said. 'Back to the dark old days of London when footpads roamed the streets and highwaymen lurked at the roadside to cut the throats of unsuspecting travellers.'

Gruesome scenes appeared on either side of the slow-moving chair. Despite the fact that Holly knew it wasn't real, she couldn't stop the hairs creeping erect on the back of her neck. Peter hadn't been exaggerating: it was very scary.

Holly wished she had been able to squeeze in with the others. She could faintly hear Miranda's voice ahead as her friend reacted to the movements of the unnervingly realistic figures in their cave-like settings in the walls.

It was the way that they came suddenly towards her that Holly found most scary; as if they were going to leap out of their sets and grab her from her seat.

A hooded figure with glowing eyes darted forwards and Holly shrank back with a stifled yelp. There was a crow of maniacal laughter from the figure as the chair swung safely past.

Holly breathed a sigh of relief, which changed into a terrified gasp as a hand snaked out from behind her, from within the chair, and clamped over her mouth. An arm came down across her chest, pinning her to her seat.

98

'Don't scream,' hissed a voice. A woman's voice close to her ear. 'I won't hurt you.'

There was a dreadful strength in those hands as Holly struggled to get loose.

'Keep still,' whispered the voice. 'I'm going to take my hand away. Don't make a sound.'

Holly nodded and the hand came away from her mouth. She twisted her head and found herself staring into the white face of Gail Farrier.

Holly gaped soundlessly at her.

'Where is it?' hissed Gail, her arm tightening across Holly's chest.

'What?' gasped Holly, alarmed by the deadly glint in Gail's eyes. 'Where's what?'

'You know what I'm talking about,' said Gail, jerking her arm up against Holly's neck. 'Tell me where it is and I won't hurt you.'

'I don't know what you're talking about,' choked Holly.

'The doll, you fool,' said Gail.

'I haven't got it,' said Holly. 'Someone took it from me.'

'You have,' Gail snarled. 'You were seen with it.'

'It was stolen,' gasped Holly.

'Don't give me that,' said Gail, staring fiercely into Holly's wide eyes. Her voice softened. 'You'd be far better off handing it over to me,' she said. 'There are other people looking for it besides me. Much worse people than me. You don't know what you've got yourself mixed up in. Just give me that doll.'

'Let me go,' said Holly. 'Let me go and I'll tell you where it is. You're choking me.' The arm relaxed slightly and Holly was able to catch her breath.

'Well?' demanded Gail.

Holly rubbed her neck. 'Why do you want it?' she asked. 'What's so important about it?'

Gail's eyes glared. 'Where is it?'

Holly shifted her feet, gathering herself. The chair crawled slowly along. It came to a corner and swung suddenly to face another dark tunnel, punctuated by the lights that glowed from the niches which held the exhibits.

It was the moment Holly had been praying for. She ducked under Gail's arm and jumped from the chair.

Gail was after her in an instant, her fingers raking down Holly's back as she ran. Blue light filled an opening in the tunnel wall just ahead. Holly stumbled over a lip of stonework, hardly having time to see where her desperate flight had taken her.

It was one of the tour's set pieces, set up to look like the inside of a darkened room. Two cloaked and hooded figures stood over a pair of waxwork victims.

Holly careered into one of the dummies and it came crashing down, tangling her in a long cloak as she tried to scramble to her feet.

She kicked out blindly, hearing a cry as her foot struck against something solid.

She was on her feet again in a moment, backing away as Gail lunged at her. She raced for the door at the back of the dimly-lit room. She caught hold of the handle. If she could only get through that door she would be able to escape.

She gave a cry of despair. The door wouldn't open. She should have realised! It was a fake room. It was a fake door.

She turned to see a look of deadly anger on Gail's face as she came towards her.

She was trapped. There was no way out.

8   The puzzle of the doll

'I wonder how Holly's getting on all on her own,' said Miranda as the chair rumbled its way slowly past the grim exhibits.

'Knowing her, she's probably taking notes,' Peter said with a laugh. 'She's probably sitting there thinking that she could have solved all these crimes twice as quickly as the police.'

'Not without us, she couldn't have,' said Belinda. She grinned at Tracy. 'Not without me, at least.' She wrinkled her nose. 'This place really stinks, doesn't it? Like an old cellar.'

'It *is* an old cellar,' said Tracy.

The chair swung round a corner.

'The Tavern Murders,' said the narration. 'The bloody corpses of the innkeeper and his wife were found one dark night in the year 1722.' In a shadowy room flickering with fake firelight two cloaked figures stood over the fallen shapes of a man and a woman in old-fashioned clothes.

'Perhaps the bill was a bit on the high side?' said Tracy, looking at the plates and tankards on the dark wood table.

'I'm surprised there was anyone left alive in the entire city,' said Belinda. 'If this is anything to go by, they must have been bumping each other off left, right and centre.'

They came to another scene. An old woman sat in a dank cellar, grinning at them.

'I don't know what you're finding so funny,' said Miranda.

The voice whispered from the roof of the chair. 'Elizabeth Brownrigg,' it told them. 'She killed four of her servant girls before being caught by the authorities and hanged in 1767.'

'Oh,' said Miranda. 'I see. Thanks for telling me.'

A piercing yell sounded from behind them, making them all jump.

Belinda laughed. 'One of Elizabeth Brownrigg's victims,' she said.

There was another yell. Tracy leaned out of the chair.

'That sounds real,' she said.

'Don't be daft,' said Peter. 'It's all part of the show.'

About five metres behind them Tracy could dimly see the following chair. The chair that Holly should have been in. Except that it was empty.

There was a third cry.

'Quick!' shouted Tracy, jumping out of the chair. 'It's Holly. There's something wrong.'

'Tracy! Are you crazy?' shouted Belinda, but Tracy was already running back down the track.

'Touch me and I'll scream,' said Holly, flinching away as Gail stepped over the fallen dummy.

'I don't want to hurt you,' said Gail. 'I just want the doll.'

'She's already got it,' Holly said desperately. Her hand was still on the fake door-handle. It wouldn't turn, but as she pressed down on it she felt it crack away from the door.

Gail's eyes narrowed. 'She? What *she*? Who do you mean?'

'You *know* who I mean,' said Holly. 'The woman you sent to Suzannah Winter's house.'

Gail stared at her. 'You're lying.'

'I don't *lie*!' shouted Holly, wrenching down on the handle, feeling it come loose in her hand. 'I'm not like *you*!' She swung her arm, throwing the missile at Gail's head.

As Gail ducked to avoid the flying handle, Holly sucked in a great lungful of air and screamed.

'Stupid!' shouted Gail. 'Stupid!'

Holly screamed again.

Anger flared in Gail's eyes, but there was desperation with it this time. She lunged forwards but Holly side-stepped her and dived to get the big old table between them.

Gathering her strength, she shoved the table towards Gail, bringing it hammering against her legs. Gail crumpled back and Holly let out a third scream.

She gasped with relief as she heard at last the sound of running feet.

A few moments later, while Gail was still struggling to her feet, Holly saw Tracy come careering into the light of the Tavern scene.

Gail scrambled up, pushing past Tracy and running down the tunnel, along the narrow path next to the track.

'Stop her!' shouted Holly.

The people in the next car along stared with open mouths as Gail's dark shape darted past with Tracy in pursuit.

Holly ran out, almost crashing into the others who had jumped out of the car to follow Tracy.

'What's going on?' shouted Miranda.

'It's Gail!' gasped Holly. 'She ran when I screamed.'

There was a sudden blaze of light and the chairs stopped.

The sound of running feet bounced off the walls as two security officers came round the corner.

'What are you kids doing?' shouted one of the guides. 'You're not supposed to get out of the chairs.'

'Someone attacked me,' said Holly. 'She ran that way.'

Tracy came trotting back down the tunnel, her cheeks red from running, her breath coming in gasps.

'She got out,' Tracy said. 'There was some kind of side exit. She's got away.'

It was clear from the faces of the two men that they thought this was some kind of joke that the five of them were playing.

'You shouldn't fool around in here,' said one of the men. 'You could've caused an accident.'

'You idiots,' said Tracy. 'We're not *pretending*!'

'We'll see about that,' said the man, frowning at her. 'Come on, all of you. Out of here.'

'Well, at least they believed us in the end,' said Belinda as they stood in the street outside the Crypt.

'They had to once they saw that side-exit door was open,' said Peter. 'I really hate it when people assume you're making things up just because you're a teenager.'

'If they'd been a bit quicker on the uptake we might have caught her,' Holly said angrily. Her throat was still sore from the pressure of Gail's arm, and she was frustrated that by the time the security guards had finally realised they were telling the truth, Gail had been given enough time to get clean away.

'I need to sit down somewhere,' said Belinda. 'This holiday is turning into a real nightmare.'

They crossed the road to a small paved area with stone benches on it.

'This wrecks all our ideas about Gail and those

other two working together, doesn't it?' said Miranda. 'If Gail is still looking for the doll, she can't know they've got it.' She sat down. 'This whole business is giving me a headache.'

'Gail said I'd been seen with the doll,' said Holly. 'But the only time I had the doll out of its bag was outside Suzannah's house.'

'Perhaps it was Gail in the car?' suggested Miranda.

'It can't have been,' said Holly. 'The other woman must have been in the car. She must have seen the doll and then followed us to the tube station. And if Gail had been with her then, she'd know they'd got it. I can't make it out.'

Belinda was walking up and down, her head lowered in thought. Suddenly she snapped her fingers and grinned.

'I've got it!' she said.

The others looked at her.

'We were right in a way,' explained Belinda. 'But we were wrong as well.'

'Terrific,' said Tracy. 'That explains *everything*.'

'Do you want to listen to me, or not?' said Belinda, frowning at her.

'Quiet, Tracy,' said Holly. She looked up at Belinda. 'Come on then, what is it?'

'We've been assuming that Gail and that other pair are working together, haven't we?' said Belinda. 'But think about it. It all makes a lot more sense if they're operating separately.'

'You saw them together,' Peter reminded her. 'Getting into the car.'

'Yes, yes,' Belinda said impatiently. 'I'm not suggesting they don't *know* each other. But I think Gail has tried to double-cross them in some way.'

'How do you make that out?' said Miranda.

'Easy,' said Belinda. 'Go right back to the beginning. These two people turn up at Suzannah's house pretending to be the police. They tell Suzannah they want to talk to Gail about something to do with drugs, and ask if they can have a look in Gail's room. Suzannah lets them, but they obviously don't find whatever it is they're looking for.'

'The doll?' said Holly.

'Possibly,' said Belinda. 'Now the fact that I saw Gail with them later must mean they *found* her. Whatever it was they wanted, she convinced them it was still in the house, so they came back for another try. When she went back with them she must have told them about the doll. That's why this other woman tried to get in later that night. They must have forced Gail to give her the key. And when that didn't work, they must have been watching the house, waiting for their chance to get their hands on the doll.'

'And they tried again at the funfair,' said Holly. 'And finally managed to get it off me on the tube train. But if they've *got* Gail, how come she doesn't know they've already stolen the doll? Why would she grab me in the Crypt?'

'Perhaps they split up,' said Belinda. 'Or perhaps Gail escaped. I don't know. But I'll bet you anything you like I'm on the right track. Gail's double-crossed them. That's *got* to be it.'

'I think you could be right,' said Peter, running his hands through his hair. 'We ought to let the police know about this.'

'No,' said Miranda, shaking her head. 'We should tell Suzannah first. The police are much more likely to believe her than us. You saw how that pair in the Crypt reacted when we told them about Holly being attacked. The police will take it seriously from Suzannah. Besides which, if Gail's still prowling about, I think Suzannah should be warned.'

'Will she be home yet?' asked Holly.

'I don't know,' said Miranda, looking at her watch. 'She might be. Or she might even be at the theatre by now.'

'I'll go to the theatre,' said Peter. 'You lot go back to her house. That way someone is bound to find her.'

'Good idea,' said Tracy. 'I'll go to the theatre with you.' She looked at the others. 'And if Suzannah isn't there we'll meet you back at her house later. OK?'

Holly stood up with a grim smile. 'At least we're getting somewhere now,' she said. She grinned at Belinda. 'What a brain!' she said.

'You know what they say,' said Peter with a

smile. 'The best detectives are the ones who think like criminals.'

Belinda gave him an affronted look. 'Are you suggesting I've got a criminal mind? Thanks a lot!'

'It was supposed to be a compliment,' said Peter.

Tracy laughed. 'With friends like Peter, you don't need enemies, do you?'

'I haven't got a criminal mind,' said Belinda. 'Holly, tell him. Tell him how honest I am.' She grinned at Peter. 'Brilliant I may be, but I'm definitely one of the good guys.'

'One of the more *conceited* good guys,' added Tracy. 'And anyway, we haven't actually *solved* anything yet.'

'Not yet,' said Holly. 'But we will!'

Suzannah's house was still empty when the three girls arrived there.

'Where can she have been all day?' asked Belinda.

'I don't know,' said Miranda. 'She's always busy. She could be anywhere. Perhaps the others will have more luck at the theatre.' Her eyes brightened. 'I know,' she said. 'I'll just nip across and see if Mrs Taylor knows anything. Suzannah quite often leaves messages with her.'

Holly and Belinda sat on the doorstep to wait for Miranda's return.

'What do you think is in the doll?' asked Belinda. 'Not drugs, you said. But what?'

'I don't know,' said Holly. 'Some secret message, perhaps? A slip of paper saying where the drugs are hidden? But I still don't see why Gail would have hidden anything in the doll in the first place.'

'In case she was caught by the other two,' said Belinda. 'Perhaps she guessed they would try and search her things once they found out she'd double-crossed them.'

'I suppose so,' said Holly. 'And then they caught up with her and forced her to tell them.'

Belinda sighed. 'I don't like the idea of us getting caught up in the middle of all this,' she said. She frowned at Holly. 'No matter where you go, something *always* happens. You're a jinx.'

'It's not my fault,' said Holly. 'You can't blame me this time.'

'No,' said Belinda. 'I suppose not.' She looked up. 'Here comes Miranda,' she said. She jumped up. 'And she's got Charlotte with her.'

The little girl was at the gate with Miranda.

'She was in with Mrs Taylor,' said Miranda. 'Suzannah had to go out all day and she left Charlotte with her.' She showed them something lying in the palm of her hand. 'It's the new door key,' she said. 'We can get in now.'

Charlotte came running up the path and caught hold of Belinda's hand.

'Have you brought Polly back?' she asked.

Belinda stroked her hair. 'I'm afraid not,' she said.

'We lost her,' said Holly. 'But we'll find her for you. Don't worry.'

'Polly will be frightened without me,' said Charlotte solemnly. 'You *will* find her, won't you?'

'It's a promise,' said Belinda. She crouched to whisper in Charlotte's ear. 'You may not know it,' she said, 'But Holly here is one of the world's best doll-finders. We'll have Polly back with you in no time.'

Miranda opened the door and they went into the house.

'Will you play horsies with me?' asked Charlotte, tugging at Belinda's arm.

'Of course,' said Belinda. 'Where's Sparky?'

'No,' said Charlotte. 'Not with Sparky. Sparky is having a rest. *You* be horsie.'

Belinda gave the others an anguished look as she was dragged into the sitting-room and pulled down on to all fours on the carpet.

'Help,' she called to them as Charlotte climbed on to her back. 'I'm being horse-napped.'

'Giddyup!' sang Charlotte, jerking her knees into Belinda's sides.

'I wouldn't have believed this if I hadn't seen it,' said Holly, watching from the sitting-room doorway as Belinda scuttled round the floor with Charlotte sitting on her back. She laughed. 'You wait 'til I tell Tracy's mother how good you are with children. She'll have you in that nursery of hers.'

Belinda made a neighing noise and waddled across the floor.

'Don't you dare,' she said. 'Anyway, horsie is hungry. Why don't you two go and get me a nosebag of something instead of standing there grinning at me?'

Miranda gave one of her wild laughs. 'I'll get some sugar lumps,' she said. 'And when Charlotte's finished we can give your mane a good brush out.'

'Ha ha,' said Belinda.

Holly and Miranda went into the hall. Miranda stood at the foot of the stairs, looking up towards the door of Gail's room.

'We could go and have a quick look, couldn't we?' she said to Holly. 'I'm sure Suzannah wouldn't mind now. Not after what's happened.'

'Tracy suggested that before,' said Holly.

'I know,' said Miranda. 'But things are a bit different now, aren't they?'

'You can say that again,' agreed Holly. 'Come on then. Let's do it.'

The two girls headed up the stairs.

The small bedroom was clean and neat. The bed was made and there was nothing obvious to show that Gail had ever been in there except for a few magazines and a meagre scattering of make-up items on the dressing-table. It looked like any other spare bedroom.

Holly opened the wardrobe. A few clothes were hanging in there and there was a large hold-all in the bottom.

Holly pulled the hold-all out on to the carpet.

'Do you think we should?' asked Miranda as Holly's fingers went to the zip.

'Yes, I do,' said Holly. 'I want to know what Gail is up to.'

The contents of the holdall were not very revealing. Just some carefully folded clothes and some spare shoes. Holly dug around under the clothes and pulled out a book. It was an ordinary street atlas of London. Spiral-bound and open to the page which showed the Highgate area.

'Look at this,' said Holly.

Miranda leaned over to see. Someone had drawn two red rings on the map.

'I know that one,' said Miranda, pointing to one of the ringed streets. 'That's the sports centre. That's where Gail does her training. You know, her dance practice.'

Holly nodded. 'Yes, I remember it,' she said. 'But what about this one?'

It was a small street on the far side of the golf course.

'Priory Close,' read Miranda. 'I don't know that area very well.'

'Gail must have ringed it for some reason,' said

Holly. She looked up at Miranda. 'It's the closest thing we've found to a clue yet.'

They heard a *thump-thump* up the stairs and Belinda came in with Charlotte clinging on to her back.

'Taking horsie for a walk,' said Charlotte. 'Why are you in Gail's room? Are you playing a trick on her?'

'No,' said Holly, standing up. 'We're just being a bit nosey, that's all.'

Charlotte climbed down off Belinda's back. 'Has Gail gone away?' she asked.

'She might have done,' said Miranda. 'We're not sure.'

'I hope she has,' said Charlotte. 'I don't like her. She hurt Polly.' She giggled. 'But I played tricks on her. Are you playing tricks on her? I can help. I'm good at tricks.'

'No,' said Miranda. 'We're not playing any tricks. We're just wondering where she could have gone.'

'What sort of tricks did you play on her, you little monkey?' asked Belinda.

Charlotte shook her head. 'Not telling,' she said. 'Mummy will be cross with me.' She pulled at Belinda's sleeve. 'Come on,' she said. 'More horsie.'

Holly looked thoughtfully at the little girl. 'How did Gail hurt Polly, Charlotte?' she asked.

But Charlotte was more interested in getting Belinda down on all fours again.

'Charlotte?' asked Holly, crouching down to the little girl's level. 'What did Gail do to hurt Polly?'

'She was nasty,' said Charlotte. 'She cut her back. I wasn't supposed to see, but I did.' Charlotte pushed her bottom lip out. 'She said she'd mend Polly, but she never did. She's a nasty woman. I'm glad she's gone away.'

'Did she hide something inside Polly?' Holly asked gently. 'Charlotte? Is that what she did?'

The shrill ringing of the doorbell sounded from the hall. Miranda crossed to the window to see who it was.

She looked round at Holly and Belinda, her face white.

'It's *them*,' she gasped. 'Gail's friends. Their car's parked outside.'

Holly ran to the window. Sure enough, parked at the kerb outside the front gate was the familiar blue car. And standing at the gate was the hard-faced woman from the tube train.

She was dressed in a police uniform.

The doorbell shrilled again as the three girls stared at one another in dismay.

9 The red circle

Holly ducked away from the window as the urgent
sound of the doorbell rang through the house. She
pressed herself against the wall, edging an eye
round the window frame to see the woman in
the police uniform come walking up the front path
of Suzannah Winter's house.

Miranda's eyes asked the question that all three
girls were thinking: *What do we do*?

'I'll go!' Charlotte chirruped happily, running out
on to the landing. 'Mummy lets me answer the door
sometimes.'

'Charlotte! No!' Belinda spun round and caught
the little girl round the waist just as she reached
the head of the stairs.

Charlotte squirmed as she was scooped up off
her feet.

'I'm *allowed* to,' she protested as Belinda carried
her back into Gail's room.

'Not this time,' said Belinda, putting her down
and taking hold of her hand. She looked at Holly
and Miranda. 'We're going to pretend we're not
in.' She knelt beside the little girl. 'We've got to

117

be really, really quiet until they go away.'

Charlotte looked puzzled. 'Why?'

'It's a game,' said Holly. 'It's a special sort of game.'

Charlotte smiled. 'Do we hide?'

Holly nodded. Charlotte ran to the bed and crouched down behind it. 'I'm hiding here,' she said.

'Good,' said Miranda. 'That's a very good place to hide. Now you've got to keep as quiet as a mouse.'

Holly glanced out of the window again. The woman had moved towards the house and was out of sight.

Across the road she saw Mrs Taylor come out of her house, heading towards her car. Holly saw her look across the road.

'She's not in, you know,' she heard Mrs Taylor call.

The woman in the police uniform reappeared on the path.

'Do you know when she'll be back?' Holly heard her ask.

'Not until late this evening,' said Mrs Taylor.

Holly heard a muffled exchange between the woman and the unseen person at the door.

'Well done, Mrs Taylor,' whispered Holly.

Mrs Taylor opened her car door. She leaned over the car roof and called again.

'The girls are probably in there, though.'

Holly groaned.

The doorbell rang again and there was the rap of the letter-box.

It could only have been a couple of minutes in reality, but it seemed like an age to the three girls before Holly dared another glance through the window. She saw the woman and the man, both in uniform, standing talking at the gate.

'No answer?' called Mrs Taylor. 'They must have taken Charlotte out somewhere.'

'Do you have any idea where they might be?' asked the man.

'In the park, possibly,' said Mrs Taylor. 'Would you like me to give Mrs Winter a message?'

'No,' said the woman. 'Thank you. We'll come back later.'

Mrs Taylor got into her car and drove away.

Holly flicked her head back as the man and woman looked towards the house.

She heard the car doors open and close but she didn't dare another look until she heard the car drive away.

'Phew!' said Belinda.

'I thought Mrs Taylor had given us away for a second there,' said Holly.

Charlotte's head popped up from behind the bed. 'Are we still hiding?' she asked.

'No,' said Miranda. 'Not any more.'

Charlotte stood up. 'Who won?'

'You did,' said Belinda.

'Are there any prizes?' asked Charlotte.

'Of course!' said Miranda. 'There are some crisps in the kitchen. The winner gets a packet of crisps. Come on.'

They went down to the kitchen.

'What were they doing here?' Holly whispered to Belinda while Miranda was helping Charlotte open her packet of crisps. 'They've *got* the doll.'

Belinda shrugged. 'Perhaps it wasn't the doll after all,' she said. 'Perhaps the stuff is hidden somewhere in the house.'

'Can I watch some television?' asked Charlotte.

'Yes, of course,' said Miranda. Charlotte trotted off to the sitting-room, leaving the three girls puzzling in the kitchen.

The ringing of the doorbell startled them. Miranda sprang up, hearing the sound of Charlotte's feet in the hall. She was answering the door. The three friends collided in the kitchen doorway as they ran to stop her.

'Hello, Charlotte. Are Holly and the others here?' It was Tracy's voice.

'Suzannah wasn't there,' said Peter as the five of them sat round the kitchen table. 'She's not expected until later this evening, so we didn't bother waiting.'

'But we did find out a bit about Gail Farrier,' added Tracy. She looked at Miranda.

'We asked Ted.'

Miranda nodded. 'Ted knows everything,' she said.

'What did you find out?' asked Holly.

'Not a great deal,' said Peter. 'Apparently no one knows all that much about her. He told us a few things we already knew. Like, Gail is a dancer and that she was staying with Suzannah while her own place was being decorated. He said she doesn't talk much to the others. She doesn't socialise with any of the rest of the cast.'

'But she travels abroad a lot,' said Tracy. 'Ted says she makes her living by being a courier when she's not being employed as a dancer.'

'What sort of courier?' asked Miranda.

'Apparently,' said Tracy, 'there are agencies which hire people to carry important parcels on airplanes. Things that they don't trust to the normal postal service. Gail does that.'

'Not drugs, surely?' asked Belinda.

'No,' said Peter. 'Legitimate things. But it would be the perfect cover for anyone who *was* trying to smuggle drugs into the country. And the really interesting thing is that Gail has only recently come back from one of these trips.'

'Where from?' asked Miranda.

'Ted didn't know,' said Tracy. 'But it was definitely somewhere abroad.'

'It fits,' Belinda said thoughtfully. 'Gail comes back from her couriering job with some illegal stuff on her, decides to keep it for herself, and hides out *here*, until she can sell it off.'

'Except that the people she's supposed to hand the stuff over to find out where she is,' said Holly. 'And they come looking for her.'

'Looking for *it*,' said Peter. 'Looking for the drugs.'

'Do you think the stuff could be hidden here?' asked Miranda. 'In the house somewhere?'

'We've had a look in Gail's room,' said Holly. 'There was nothing obvious.'

'She wouldn't hide it anywhere *obvious*,' said Tracy.

'And it's definitely not in the doll,' said Belinda. 'That pair of crooks wouldn't have come back here if they'd found anything in the doll.'

'We can't search the entire house,' said Miranda. 'But we could have a more careful look in Gail's room. See if there are any loose floorboards or anything.'

They went quietly upstairs. They could hear the sound of the television from the front room. At least that would keep Charlotte busy while they searched.

They spent an hour or more painstakingly going over every inch of the room. Under the carpet, behind furniture, beneath the mattress. Everywhere. There was no sign of anything that looked remotely illegal.

'The only thing we found was this,' Holly

showed Peter and Tracy the London atlas with its red-ringed streets.

'I wonder what she circled this one for,' said Tracy, pointing towards the ring that was drawn around Priory Close.

'Perhaps that's where she lives,' suggested Miranda.

Tracy shook her head. 'She wouldn't need to highlight her own house,' she said. 'It's got to be something else.'

'Perhaps it was where she was supposed to meet up with that other pair to hand over the stuff,' said Belinda. 'That would make more sense.'

'I'm hungry!' They looked round as they heard Charlotte's voice calling up the stairs.

'Teatime,' said Miranda. She looked at her watch. 'Well past her teatime, actually. Anyone hungry?'

'I am,' said Belinda. 'I never got those sugar lumps you promised me.'

Miranda laughed. 'And we never brushed your mane.'

'Forget that,' said Belinda. 'Just lead me to the food.'

They made their way down to the kitchen.

'What are we going to do, though?' asked Peter. 'I mean, what's the next logical step?'

'I think we should go to Priory Close,' said Holly. 'We could have a look round, at least.'

'We can't leave Charlotte,' said Miranda.

'I could go,' said Peter.

'Not without the rest of us you can't,' said Tracy.

'But it might be dangerous,' said Peter. 'Who knows what might be there?'

Tracy stared at him. 'I see,' she said. 'The big brave boy goes while all the girls hide back here? No way!'

'It was just a suggestion,' said Peter.

'No one's going without me,' said Miranda. 'We'll just have to wait until Suzannah gets home.'

'It might be getting dark by then,' said Holly. 'I don't fancy nosing around some strange place in the dark, not knowing who or what might jump out at us. I had enough of that in the Crypt.'

'We could go first thing tomorrow,' said Tracy. She looked pointedly at Peter. 'All of us.'

'OK, is that agreed?' said Holly. 'First thing in the morning, then.'

They all agreed, and then set about preparing a meal for themselves and Charlotte.

'I hope Suzannah doesn't mind having her fridge raided like this,' said Belinda. 'I bet she wasn't counting on having to feed this many mouths.'

'She won't mind,' said Miranda. 'I'm doing her a big favour anyway. This isn't one of my proper baby-sitting nights. I only agreed to take Charlotte because Mrs Taylor said she had to go off somewhere urgently. The least Suzannah can do is feed us all.'

Charlotte was in bed and the five friends were

sitting talking over events and half-watching the television when there was a ring at the door.

'It's them again!' Belinda said in alarm. It was going to be difficult to pretend the house was deserted now that the lights were on.

Miranda peered through the side window. 'No, it isn't,' she said. 'It's Mrs Taylor.'

She went to answer the door. Mrs Taylor came into the sitting-room.

'It's very good of you to have taken Charlotte on at such short notice.' She looked round at them. 'Although you seem to have made a bit of a party of it. Does it usually take five of you to look after her?'

'It does when one of you is the horse,' said Belinda.

Mrs Taylor gave her a bemused look.

'Anyway, I've got some good news for you,' said Mrs Taylor. 'Suzannah just phoned me. She's not going to be back until very late, so I'll take Charlotte over to my house for the night.'

The five friends tidied up, gathered their things and headed off for Miranda's house. They stopped on the corner where Peter was to leave them to go home.

'I'll see you all tomorrow, then,' he said. 'First thing.'

Belinda gave a sigh. 'Does it have to be *first* thing? What's wrong with *second* thing?'

'*First* thing,' said Holly firmly. 'At nine o'clock tomorrow morning we go to Priory Close. And with any luck we'll find out why Gail circled it on the map.'

Peter arrived at Miranda's house at exactly nine o'clock the following morning.

Priory Close was about two kilometres away from where Miranda lived and Belinda insisted they catch a bus.

'I'm not walking all that way,' she said. 'I want some strength left for some sightseeing later. You realise we've been here three days, and all we've done is a bus tour and a quick look round Covent Garden.'

'And the Crypt,' said Miranda. 'Don't forget that.'

'I wish I could,' said Belinda.

'Never mind,' said Miranda. 'Don't forget we're off to the theatre this evening to see *The Snow Queen.*'

'What are we going to do if we find anything this morning?' asked Peter.

'Tell Suzannah,' said Miranda. 'Then she can tell the police.' She grinned. 'We'll be heroes. Busting a drugs ring like that.'

'*If* we find anything,' Belinda reminded her. 'I've been on Holly's wild goose chases before.'

They got off the bus and headed down the long road that led to Priory Close, Holly consulting the sketch-map she had drawn in the Mystery Club's red notebook.

'It's about halfway down this street, on the right,' she told them.

'Aren't we a bit conspicuous?' said Miranda. 'All five of us, I mean? We're hardly going to be able to hide behind a lamppost if someone spots us.'

'Let's see what's there before we worry about that,' said Holly.

They came to a narrow turning that dived down between the rows of terraced houses.

'This is it,' said Holly. 'You wait here. I'll go down for a quick look, then report back.'

She pushed the notebook into her pocket and walked cautiously into the side street.

The roadway was only wide enough for a single car to pass. On one side a blank, brick wall screened the view. On the other side, the road opened out into a tarmac area and a row of lock-up garages. There was nothing else. The road ended in a wooden fence which hemmed in tall trees.

She came back to the others and told them what she had seen.

'Was the car there?' asked Belinda.

'Not on the road,' said Holly. 'It looks completely deserted.'

'It sounds like the sort of place where people might meet to hand over something illegal,' said Peter. 'An out-of-the-way place where they couldn't be seen. Are we going to investigate, or what?'

'Investigate what?' asked Belinda. 'Holly's already said there's nothing there.'

127

'What about *inside* one of the garages?' said Tracy. 'Their car might be in one of them. If we find *that*, the police will be able to stake the place out and catch them when they come for it.'

'The garages will all be locked up,' said Holly.

'We should still *look*,' insisted Tracy. 'This is the only clue we've got. We can't just drop it. Come on.' She walked into the street and the others followed her.

'See?' said Holly. 'There's no way of getting inside.'

'What about round the back?' suggested Peter. He pointed to a narrow gap between the row of garages and the back wall of a house. 'There are bound to be air vents or something that we could see in through.'

They filed along the gap, coming out into an unkempt slope of rubble and tall weeds. The back walls of the garages were of blank brick.

Peter scrambled up the slope and stood on tiptoe.

'There are skylights,' he said. 'In the roofs. If someone gave me a leg up, I could probably see down through them.'

'You'll fall through and break your neck,' said Miranda.

'No, I won't,' said Peter. 'Not if I'm careful. The roofs look solid enough.'

'I'll do it,' said Tracy. 'I'm lighter than you.'

Peter stood against the wall and cupped his hands. Spreading her arms out against the brick-work, Tracy levered herself up. She caught hold of the edge and dragged herself on to the roof.

She looked down at the waiting faces. 'It's filthy up here,' she said.

'Never mind about that,' said Holly. 'Can you see anything?'

Tracy crawled to the rim of the skylight. The glass was caked with grime. She rubbed a corner and peered through. In the gloomy well of the interior she saw piles of rubbish and a dismantled motorbike.

'Nothing in here,' she called. She crawled along to the next skylight, the other four scrambling through the weeds to keep level with her.

'No go,' she called again. 'And I'm getting into a real state up here.'

'Stop moaning,' said Belinda. 'You volunteered for the job.'

The next three garages were all the same. Two of them held cars, but not the car they were looking for.

'How's it going?' called Peter.

'Hold everything!' Tracy shouted excitedly. 'I think this is it.' She rubbed the corner of the skylight and doubled over, staring down into the dimness. 'Yes!' she said. She could see the shape of a blue car. 'At least, I *think* it's the one. It's difficult to tell. The glass is real dirty.'

129

'Stay there,' said Peter. 'I'm coming up. Holly, give me a lift, will you?'

Holly braced herself as Peter put his foot into her cupped hands and hoisted himself up the wall. His legs swung as he struggled to pull himself on to the roof.

'Ow!' Holly exclaimed. 'That was my head!'

'Sorry,' said Peter, squirming on to the flat of the roof.

He crawled over to where Tracy was kneeling.

'We'll see better if we can get this open,' he said. He scrabbled at the wooden frame. Slivers of wood came away under his fingers.

'It's fairly rotten,' he said. 'If I can just get my fingers under here.' He brushed away the crumbling pieces of wood and jammed his fingers into the narrow gap.

'Give me a bit of room,' said Tracy, edging him aside so that she could get her own fingers under the frame.

'Right,' she said. 'One, two three . . . heave!'

'Got it!' said Peter, as the skylight opened. 'Well done.'

'I'm not completely feeble,' said Tracy. The skylight opened about half a metre then stopped.

'There's a bar on the inside,' said Tracy, looking through the slot. 'It won't let it open any more.'

Peter held the skylight open as Tracy leaned into the gap.

'I can get through,' said Tracy. 'There's some

kind of metal shelving. If I can just get my foot on to it, I'll be able to climb right down.'

It was not much more than a two metre drop down into the interior of the garage. There were wooden boxes and other pieces of debris scattered about the floor.

'Careful,' said Peter as Tracy lowered herself through the hole.

'No problem,' said Tracy. 'I'm – *oops!*' The rusty shelving unit groaned under her weight and shifted alarmingly.

She vanished suddenly and there was a crash from within the garage.

'Are you OK?' called Peter.

'Yes. Fine,' said Tracy. 'I slipped, that's all. I haven't hurt myself.'

'I'm coming down,' said Peter.

'Be careful then,' Tracy warned him as he eased himself through the slim gap and stretched down, his toes finding the edge of the top shelf. The skylight thudded closed above him as Tracy held the rocking unit steady for him to make his way down the metal shelves.

'It's the right car, OK,' said Peter. 'And look in here.'

Tracy looked through the side window. On the back seat they could see dark blue clothes and the faint glint of silver buttons.

'It's the police uniforms,' said Tracy.

'Right,' said Peter, moving round to the front

of the car. 'I'll give them something to think about.'

'What are you doing?'

Peter was feeling along under the front of the bonnet.

'It's a little trick I picked up,' he said. 'Watch.' There was a click and the bonnet sprang up. 'I'm going to disable the car,' he said. 'That'll slow them down. I only need to disconnect a couple of wires.'

Tracy grinned. 'How do you know how to do that?' she said.

'That would be telling,' said Peter, leaning in under the raised bonnet.

Tracy walked round the side of the car. She stopped, seeing something lying on the floor.

'Peter, look!' she said, picking the thing up.

Peter stood up, wiping his hands on his jeans as he walked over to her.

It was Charlotte's doll. The dress had been wrenched up and the back seam was torn open, the stuffing hanging out in clumps.

'They've torn it apart,' said Peter. 'They must have been looking for something.'

'So Belinda was wrong when she thought there was nothing in the doll after all,' said Tracy.

At that moment they heard a frantic hiss from the skylight. Against the white of the sky they saw the dark shape of Holly's head.

'Quick! Get up out of there,' she hissed. 'They're coming. Both of them.'

They ran round to the back of the car.

'You first,' Tracy said urgently to Peter, taking hold of the shelving unit to steady it for Peter's climb. 'Then you can lean through the skylight and hold it for me.'

Peter climbed, pushing the skylight open. His legs had just disappeared through the narrow slot and he was squirming round to lean back in when they heard the sound of someone unlocking the garage door.

'Quick!' whispered Peter, reaching precariously down to try and get a grip on the unit.

Tracy glanced round towards the door.

A crack of light appeared. There was no time for her to get out. She was going to be caught in there.

10 Charlotte's secret

Tracy had just enough time to gesture to Peter to close the skylight and duck for cover behind the shelving unit before she heard the scrape of the garage door being opened. A wash of daylight came into the garage as the single door was lifted and clanged noisily against the roof.

Tracy crouched against the cold back wall. Unless they actually came right over there and looked around behind the metal unit she would be safe. For the time being at least.

'I'm getting sick and tired of all this play-acting,' Tracy heard the man say. 'That Farrier woman has played us for fools once too often. I say we just get into that house, find the key, and get out. All that rubbish she gave us about the doll. The key was never in there, I'm telling you.'

'It's your fault she managed to get away from us after we'd seen that girl with the doll,' said the woman. 'If you'd listened to me, we'd have her locked up safe and sound right now.' Her voice lowered menacingly. 'I'd have got the truth out of her. I never trusted her. She won't get away from us a second time.'

'Forget her,' said the man. 'We can deal with Gail Farrier later. I'm more concerned about getting our hands on that key. It must be in the house. I told you we should have broken in there last night.'

'Don't be so stupid,' said the woman. 'That land-lady of hers still believes we're from the police. She let us in before. She'll cooperate again. We know what we're looking for this time.'

'And if we don't find it?' asked the man. 'What then?'

'We'll find it one way or another,' said the woman darkly. 'It's in there somewhere, if we have to tear the place apart to find it. And if we get any trouble from that Winter woman we'll just have to deal with her, won't we?'

A chill ran down Tracy's spine. The tone in the woman's voice suggested that their way of dealing with anyone who got in their way would be very brutal.

'Come on,' said the man. 'We've wasted too much time as it is, pussyfooting around. I want that stuff by tonight, whatever we have to do to get it.'

'We'll have it,' said the woman. 'And then we'll find Gail and show her what happens to people who double-cross us.'

Tracy heard one of them get into the car. There were a few feeble spluttering noises from the engine.

135

'Get on with it,' said the woman. 'What are you playing at?'

The car door banged open. 'I'm not playing at anything,' said the man. 'The car won't start.' The engine coughed and spluttered a few more times.

'Can't you fix it?' the woman said angrily.

'Do you think I'd be sitting here if I knew how to fix it?' snarled the man. There were a few more plaintive sounds from the engine. 'I don't know what's wrong with it,' said the man.

'We'll have to do without it,' said the woman. 'We'll use my car.'

'The police don't use cars like yours,' said the man. 'That was the whole point of stealing this one.'

'We can park it out of sight of the house,' said the woman. Tracy heard the sound of the car door being slammed. The man was getting out.

'Get the uniforms,' said the woman. 'We can change at my place.' Tracy heard the distinct sound of the car being kicked. 'This whole thing has been a fiasco ever since we missed Gail at the house that night.'

'Calm down,' said the man. 'It'll all be sorted by tonight.'

Tracy crouched perfectly still as she listened to the sounds of the two people moving about in the garage. Then there came the scrape of the garage door being closed and the garage was plunged once more into darkness.

Tracy let out a gasp of relief and stood up, cautiously looking out from her hiding-place. She tucked the ruined doll into her shirt and was just about to start climbing up the shelves when the skylight opened and a shaft of sunlight illuminated her face.

'Tracy?' It was Peter's voice. 'Are you OK?'

'Yes. Hold the shelves steady for me, will you?'

Peter reached down and kept the shelving unit from moving as Tracy climbed up and slid through the narrow gap on to the roof. They jumped down to where their friends were waiting.

'It was a good job I thought to keep a look out,' said Belinda. 'I'd only just poked my nose out when I saw them coming. I thought they'd get you for sure in there.'

'No way,' said Tracy, her eyes gleaming. 'And I know what was supposed to be in the doll.' She drew the doll out to show them. 'They were talking about it. It wasn't drugs. It was a key. Gail must have told them she'd locked the stuff away somewhere and that she'd hidden the key in the doll. They're going back there now, to look for it.' She grinned round at Peter. 'At least they *would* be if Peter hadn't fixed their car. They said they were going back to the woman's place to change. That should give us time to get to Suzannah's house and warn her.' Tracy clapped her hands together in glee. 'We'll be able to have the police waiting for them.'

'But what about the key?' asked Miranda. 'Or do you think that was all nonsense? I suppose Gail could have made it up to stall them.'

'I don't think so,' said Holly. 'I think the key *was* in there. Remember how the stitching was all undone down the back before?'

'So where is it now?' asked Belinda. 'Gail hasn't got it. And neither have those two.'

'Perhaps it fell out somewhere in the house,' said Holly. 'Let's get back there. Now!'

Miranda opened the front door with her new key.

'Suzannah?' she called. 'Charlotte? Anyone?'

Mrs Taylor came out of the sitting-room.

'Hello,' said Miranda. 'I wasn't expecting to see you here.'

'Suzannah asked me to look after Charlotte,' said Mrs Taylor. 'She had to go out on business. But what are *you* doing here?' She looked questioningly at Miranda as the hall filled with people.

Charlotte came running down the stairs.

'Have you found Polly?' she cried.

Holly held up the bedraggled doll. 'Yes,' she said. 'And she's had lots of adventures.'

With a whoop of joy the little girl grabbed the doll out of Holly's hands. Her face fell as she saw the tear down the back seam and the stuffing hanging out.

'We'll fix her,' said Miranda. 'She'll be as good as new.' She looked at Mrs Taylor. 'We can take over, if you like. When is Suzannah expected back?'

'Not before tonight,' said Mrs Taylor. 'I said I could look after Charlotte until then, but if you really don't mind taking over from me, I'd be very grateful.'

'That's fine,' said Miranda. 'We'll look after Charlotte. No problem.'

Mrs Taylor smiled at the five of them. 'I'll be off then,' she said. 'I'll leave you to it.'

Miranda closed the door after her.

'Are you all going to play with me?' Charlotte asked brightly.

'We certainly are,' said Belinda. 'All five of us.' She gave Peter a meaningful look. 'Peter particularly likes playing horsie, don't you, Peter?'

'Do I?' said Peter, looking uneasily at Charlotte. 'But I'm filthy.'

'Me too,' said Tracy, with a grin. Both of them showed the grimy evidence of their exploits up on the garage roof. 'Let's go and wash, then Peter can be horsie.'

A few minutes later, when they came back down, Belinda dragged Peter into the sitting-room.

'Come on, Charlotte,' she said. 'Let's show Peter how horsie is played.' She looked round at the others. 'And you lot,' she whispered, 'can figure out what we do *now*.'

'What do we do?' asked Tracy. 'Those crooks

could be here any time. We can't wait for Suzannah to get back.'

'We wait for them,' said Holly. 'And at the first sign of them we get on the phone to the police.'

They went into the sitting-room. A very forlorn-looking Peter was lumbering about on all fours with Charlotte sitting on his back.

'Come on, horsie,' Belinda laughed. 'Do your stuff.'

'And I'll see if I can find a needle and thread to sew poor old Polly up again,' said Holly.

'Had Gail stolen her?' asked Charlotte.

'Well, not exactly,' said Miranda. 'But I think she had something to do with it.' She smiled at Charlotte. 'But not to worry, she's back now, isn't she?'

Charlotte nodded cheerfully. 'I'm glad I played those tricks on her,' she said. 'Bad woman. Putting things in Polly's back.'

There was a short silence as the five friends took this in.

'What things?' asked Holly.

Charlotte put both hands over her mouth. 'Mustn't tell,' she said. 'Mummy will be cross.'

'Was it a key, Charlotte?' Belinda asked gently. 'Did Gail put a key in Polly's back?'

Charlotte grinned, kicking Peter's sides with her heels. 'Ride, horsie,' she said.

Belinda lifted Charlotte off Peter's back and sat down with her in her lap.

'You can tell *us*,' said Belinda. 'We won't give it away.'

Charlotte clasped her hands together in her lap, staring down at the floor with her lower lip out.

'Yes,' she said softly. 'It was a key. But I took it out again and hid it so Gail wouldn't be able to find it.' She glanced at Belinda. 'Was I naughty?'

'No,' said Belinda. 'Gail was naughty for putting it in there in the first place.' She gave Charlotte a hug. 'Now,' she said. 'Would you like to tell us where you hid it?'

Charlotte shook her head. 'It's a secret,' she said quietly.

Miranda crouched at her side. 'We won't let on,' she said. 'You can tell us, can't you?'

Charlotte shook her head again, her chin tucked into her dress front.

'I'll tell you something,' Tracy said, smiling encouragingly at Charlotte. 'My mom runs a nursery up where I live. Sometimes we play hide-and-seek. Why don't we play a game of hide-and-seek now, Charlotte? You don't have to tell us where the key is. Just say if we're getting warm. How's that sound? Fun, huh?'

Charlotte's face cleared and she smiled and nodded.

'OK,' said Tracy. 'Are we warm right now?'

Charlotte shook her head. 'Cold,' she said. 'Ever so cold.'

They went into various downstairs rooms.

141

'Cold! Cold! Cold!' shouted Charlotte.

'Upstairs, then?' said Holly.

'I bet it's in your room, isn't it?' said Miranda, running up the stairs.

'Warm!' yelled Charlotte, following them up.

They stood in Charlotte's chaotic bedroom. Peter stared at the mess.

'This could take hours,' he whispered to Holly.

'Is it in here?' asked Tracy.

'Not telling,' said Charlotte. 'But you're warm. Warmer than before.'

Belinda and Miranda picked their way across the floor, their hands outstretched.

'Warmer,' chuckled Charlotte. 'Belinda's warmest.'

Belinda was by the windowsill with its row of piggy banks.

She looked round at Charlotte, grinning. 'I've got it!' she said. She lifted the Secret Pig from the shelf.

'Hot!' shouted Charlotte.

Belinda rattled the pig and once again heard the solitary clank from within. She laughed, turning the pig on to its back and easing out the plastic stopper.

She tipped the pig and a key fell into her hand.

'Belinda wins!' crowed Charlotte, jumping up and down. 'Belinda's won!'

They were back in the sitting-room, the key on the coffee table in front of them. Charlotte was sitting contentedly on the couch eating an ice-cream that Miranda had got her from the freezer as a reward for being good.

It was a small key, smaller than an ordinary door key. It had a little plastic tag attached to the grip. Stencilled on the tag were the numbers 327.

'It's got to be for a briefcase or some sort of box,' said Holly. 'But *where*?'

'Somewhere in the house?' suggested Peter. He looked at Miranda. 'Have you ever seen a briefcase around here?'

Miranda shook her head. 'It's not that sort of key,' she said. 'Not for a brief-case. That wouldn't have a number on it, surely?'

'It's got to be for somewhere where there are a lot of lockable places,' said Holly.

'I know what it reminds me of,' said Tracy. 'It's like the keys we have for the lockers in the gym back at school. They've all got numbers on them like that.'

Belinda sat bolt upright. 'That's it!' she said. 'You've done it again! I don't know how anyone with a brain the size of a walnut can keep coming up with ideas the way you do, Tracy.'

'Excuse me,' Tracy said in annoyance. 'I don't have a brain the size of a walnut.' She frowned at Belinda. 'And what exactly have I done now?'

Belinda looked excitedly at Miranda. 'What did you say that other place was that Gail had ringed in the street atlas?'

'A sports centre,' said Miranda. 'Gail uses it for dance practice, but – oh!' She stared at the key. 'The sports centre!' she breathed.

'Exactly!' said Belinda, looking triumphantly round at the others. 'The sports centre!'

Holly clutched the key in her fist as she, Peter and Tracy got off the bus. The smooth glass and brick front of the sports centre towered above them beyond a wide white pavement.

They had left Belinda and Miranda to look after Charlotte, promising to telephone them the moment they had found out what was inside the locker.

It finally felt to Holly that they were on the brink of solving the entire mystery. Whatever it was that Gail had brought back from her recent trip abroad, Holly felt sure its secret would be revealed beyond those dark glass doors.

They went up the broad steps and came into a high-tech reception area, all shining metal and tinted glass.

There was a board on the far wall, pointing the way to the gym and the swimming-pools and the squash courts.

'We could do with a place like this in Willow Dale,' said Tracy, her eyes wide as she looked round. 'I could spend half my *life* in there.'

'Here we are,' said Peter, reading the board. 'Dance class. Third floor. That'll be it.'

They made their way up the stairs, keeping their eyes on the signboards as they headed for the third floor.

A few people were wandering about in leotards and shorts, but no one challenged them as they came up to the correct floor and walked in the direction that the sign pointed.

Holly pushed open a set of double swing-doors. A wall confronted them. There were two signs, pointing in opposite directions: Women's Changing Area and Men's Changing Area.

'I guess it's going to be this way,' said Tracy, gesturing in the direction of the Women's Changing Area. She looked at Peter. 'You'll have to wait here.'

'Come straight back,' said Peter.

'We will,' said Holly. 'Don't worry.'

The two girls followed the wall to another set of swing-doors. The room beyond was lined with grey metal lockers. From the far side of another set of doors they could hear music and rhythmic thuddings. A voice sounded above the noise, shouting instructions.

The lockers were numbered.

'Here,' said Tracy, running her fingers across the lockers as she read out the numbers. '120. 121.' She looked round. 'It must be on the other side.'

'Got it,' said Holly.

Tracy stood behind her as she slid the key into the lock.

Holly grinned round at her. 'It fits!' she said.

'Open it, for heaven's sake!' said Tracy.

Holly turned the key and pulled the door open. A leotard, leggings and a pair of dance shoes met her eyes. She pulled them aside. There, deep in the back of the locker, was a dark plastic bundle.

She pulled it out.

It was a plastic bag. She unwrapped it and looked inside.

'Well?' said Holly.

'I don't know,' said Holly, reaching into the bag. She drew out a newspaper-wrapped package about the size of a bag of sugar.

'It's quite heavy,' she said.

They heard a sharp hiss from behind them. Peter's head had appeared round the swing-doors. 'What have you found?' he whispered.

The two girls went over to him and the three of them stood in the corridor, staring down at the mysterious package in its wrap of newspaper.

'Open it,' Tracy said impatiently. 'Oh, give it to me.'

She took the package out of Holly's hands and eagerly unfolded the newspaper.

'What on earth . . .?'

The three of them stared down at what had been revealed.

It was a large slab of soft clay-like stuff.

'Drugs?' said Holly uncertainly. 'Is it?'

'Don't drugs usually come like powder or pills?'

146

said Tracy. 'This stuff is more like modelling clay.'

'Holly,' said Peter softly. 'Put the package down.'
Holly glanced at him. There was a strange, choking tone in his voice, and his eyes were wide.

'Why?' asked Holly.

'Just *do* it,' said Peter. 'I think I know what that stuff is. I've seen stuff just like it on television. It's not drugs, Holly. It's plastic explosive.'

Holly's head swam as she looked down at the slab of stuff that lay across her hands.

She glanced at Tracy, who was backing slowly away from her.

'Help,' said Holly softly. She didn't dare move a muscle. She hardly dared breathe.

11 Revelations

Miranda was kneeling on the couch, leaning over the back to look out of Suzannah Winter's sitting-room window. By the door, Belinda sat with the telephone in her lap, ready at a word from Miranda to call for help.

They had settled Charlotte in her room with poster paints and paper. They wanted her to be well out of the way when the two fake police officers turned up.

The afternoon was wearing away.

'Shouldn't they be here by now?' asked Belinda. 'It's been *hours*.'

Miranda glanced round at her. 'Perhaps they had an accident on the way here,' she said. She gave a bleak laugh. 'It would serve them right if they had.'

'Wishful thinking,' said Belinda, grinning round at her. 'Things never work out *quite* that conveniently.' She stared out into the street. 'I hope something happens soon. Do you think it's worth phoning the theatre? Suzannah might be there by now.'

'Yes,' said Miranda. 'Do that. The number's pinned to the board in the hall.'

Belinda listened for a few moments to the engaged tone, then put the receiver down.

'I hope this doesn't mean we're going to miss the show tonight,' said Belinda.

Miranda groaned. 'I'd completely forgotten it was tonight,' she said. 'Perhaps one of us should go over to the theatre now and find Suzannah? I wish Holly would phone to let us know if they've found anything at the sports centre. Just sitting about like this is driving me nuts.'

'You go,' said Belinda. 'I'll stay here with Charlotte.'

'Will you be all right on your own?' asked Miranda.

'Of course,' said Belinda. 'I can keep watch from here. Perhaps you could take Charlotte up some crisps before you go? She'll be getting hungry soon, and I don't want that pair to arrive while I'm making her something to eat.'

Miranda nodded and went upstairs. A few seconds later Belinda heard her come racing down the stairs.

'She's not there,' cried Miranda. 'She's not in her room.'

Belinda scrambled to her feet, her stomach turning over.

'The kitchen?' she suggested, her face white.

They ran through into the kitchen, but there was

no sign of Charlotte in there either.

'She can't have *gone* anywhere,' said Belinda. 'She must be in the house somewhere.' She gave a sudden breathless laugh, pointing to the back door. It was slightly ajar. 'She's in the garden,' she said.

Miranda pushed the door open. Charlotte was right down at the bottom of the garden by the fence. She wasn't alone. Crouched in front of her was the unmistakable figure of Gail Farrier.

Miranda let out a shout.

Gail sprang up and leaped for the fence, vaulting over it and disappearing into the alleyway beyond.

Belinda and Miranda ran down the garden. Charlotte didn't seem upset. She was clutching a bag of sweets.

Miranda jumped at the fence, pulling herself up. Gail had already run out of sight. With a gasp Miranda dropped back into the garden.

'She gave me these,' said Charlotte, holding the bag of sweets out. 'She said she was sorry.'

'What did she want?' asked Belinda, trying to keep her voice calm so that she didn't alarm the little girl.

'She said she wanted to mend Polly,' said Charlotte. 'She wanted me to bring Polly out for her to mend.' She looked up at Belinda with big eyes. 'I told her about the tricks I'd played on her.'

'Did you tell her we'd found the key?' asked

Miranda.

Charlotte nodded solemnly. 'And I told her about the other thing.'

'What other thing?' asked Belinda.

'The bag of stuff that I hid,' said Charlotte. 'I told her where I hid it.'

'What bag?' asked Miranda. 'Charlotte, please, this is important. What bag are you talking about?'

'She had a bag in her room,' said Charlotte. 'I saw her with it. You won't tell Mummy what I did, will you?'

'Tell us first what you did with the bag, Charlotte,' said Miranda. 'You won't get into trouble, I promise.'

'It was in a plastic bag,' said Charlotte. 'Wrapped up in newspaper in another plastic bag. I took it and put my Plasticine in there instead.' She frowned. 'She called me Lottie. I wanted to pay her back.' She looked anxiously up at them. 'I didn't mean to keep it,' she said. 'I would have given it back.'

'Of course, you would,' said Belinda. 'But what did you do?'

'I wrapped my Plasticine up in the newspaper and put it back in the bag.' She shook her head. 'But she didn't look. I was going to swap it back afterwards but the bag had gone.'

'What was in the bag that you took out?' asked Belinda.

'I don't know what it was,' said Charlotte. 'It

looked like make-up stuff, like Mummy uses. A plastic bag of white powder stuff.'

'You've been very good to tell us this,' said Belinda. 'Now, what did you do with the bag of powder?'

'I hid it in Mummy's case.'

'Can you show us?' asked Miranda.

Charlotte shook her head.

'No one's cross with you,' said Miranda. 'But you must show us where you put the bag, Charlotte. It's very, very important.'

'It's in Mummy's case,' said Charlotte. 'I hid it right down at the bottom. In Mummy's work case. The one she takes to work.'

Miranda and Belinda stared at each other.

'The make-up case,' said Miranda. 'Remember? We saw it in Suzannah's dressing-room.' She looked down at Charlotte. 'You're sure that's where you put it?'

Charlotte nodded.

'OK,' said Miranda. 'Let's go and phone your mummy.' She took Charlotte's hand. 'Don't worry,' she said. 'She won't be cross with you.'

The theatre was still engaged. Miranda slammed the phone down.

'We've got to get there before Gail does,' she said. 'I'll go. You stay here with Charlotte.'

'No,' said Belinda. 'I'm coming with you.' She looked down at Charlotte. 'Would you like to go with us to see your mummy?'

Charlotte nodded.

'We'll leave a note for Holly and the others,' said Miranda. She quickly scribbled a message on a sheet of paper.

Gone to theatre. Found where the stuff is. Meet us there.

Miranda opened the front door and slid the sheet of paper under the mat, leaving one corner showing.

'Holly's pretty quick on the uptake,' she said. 'When no one answers the door she's bound to spot it.'

'OK,' said Belinda, taking Charlotte's hand. 'Let's go.'

They were about to close the front door behind them when Belinda suddenly pushed them back into the house.

'It's them!' she hissed, closing the door. She had seen the man and woman walking along towards the house dressed as police officers.

'Quick,' said Miranda. 'Let's get out. Over the back wall.'

'Are we playing another game?' asked Charlotte as they ran through the kitchen.

'That's right,' said Belinda. 'Cops and robbers. We're the goodies and we're pretending we've got to escape from some baddies.'

As they ran down the garden they heard the doorbell ring.

'The note for Holly,' gasped Miranda. 'They'll see it!'

'We can't help that,' said Belinda. She climbed the fence, straddling the top as Miranda lifted Charlotte into her arms. Belinda lowered the little girl into the alley and the three of them ran.

They paused on the pavement.

'What's the quickest way to get to the theatre?' asked Belinda.

Miranda gave a shout and waved her arm. It was the best piece of real luck they could have wished for. A black taxi was coming along the road.

It pulled into the kerb.

'Hampstead Gardens Theatre,' said Miranda as they tumbled into the taxi. 'As quick as you can, please!'

Holly lowered herself slowly to a crouch, bringing the pale grey slab in its crumple of newspaper down to the floor. Peter and Tracy watched her with wildly thudding hearts.

'Careful,' whispered Tracy. 'Careful!'

Holly slid her hands out from under the parcel and stood up again, backing against the wall.

All eyes focused on the innocent-looking lump of stuff that they had taken from Gail's locker.

'Now what?' whispered Holly.

'Get help,' said Peter.

'Wait,' said Tracy. 'Just wait a minute. What exactly sets plastic explosive off? I mean, what makes it explode?'

154

'I think it needs a detonator,' said Peter. 'Some kind of electrical charge.'

'That's right,' said Holly. 'Like you see in the films.'

'So does that mean it can't blow up in our faces?' asked Tracy, her voice shaking.

'I'm not sure,' said Peter. 'Tracy! What are you doing?'

Tracy had got down on all fours and was edging towards the package. 'I want to take a closer look,' she said. She reached out to push down the crumpled paper. 'There's something screwy here,' she said. 'Look.'

Peter and Holly glanced fearfully at each other.

'Tracy, don't!' gasped Holly as Tracy lifted the slab of stuff up.

'Have you ever heard of multicoloured plastic explosives?' she said with a breathless laugh. She held the slab up to them. Under the top layer of grey, the stuff was formed of several different coloured layers. Blue, red, green, yellow; all pressed together.

'It's Plasticine!' cried Tracy, crumpling against the wall with a pant of relieved laughter.

'What?' Holly stared at it, and then at Peter. 'Peter! You idiot.'

'Plasticine!' laughed Tracy.

Peter gave them a shamefaced grin. 'It *looked* like plastic explosives,' he said.

Tracy broke the slab in half. 'Anyone want to do a bit of modelling?'

155

Holly frowned at Peter. 'If you ever frighten me like that again, I'll murder you!' she said.

'But why would Gail hide a lump of Plasticine away in a locker?' said Peter. 'It doesn't make sense.'

'Oh, yes, it does,' said Holly. 'It was Charlotte.'

'Charlotte?' said Tracy. 'How does Charlotte fit in?'

'Don't you remember?' said Holly. 'Charlotte said she played *tricks* on Gail. Not *a* trick. Tricks!'

'She must have swapped the real stuff for the Plasticine without Gail knowing,' said Tracy.

Peter nodded. 'And Gail never thought to check before she brought it here.' He looked at his friends. 'So where's the real stuff?'

'Charlotte must have hidden it somewhere in the house,' said Holly. 'We'd better get back there.'

'No,' said Peter. 'We can phone from here.'

They ran down to the reception area and found a pay-phone.

'Come on, come on,' urged Holly as the ringing tone sounded, unanswered, from Suzannah's house.

'They couldn't have gone out,' said Tracy. 'Something must have happened. Maybe those people got them. They could be in real trouble, Holly.'

'I know, I know,' said Holly. 'But it'll take us half an hour to get back there. Anything could happen in that amount of time.'

'We could get to the theatre quicker,' said Peter.

'It's only a few streets away from here. If we take the short cut across the gardens we could be there in ten minutes. Suzannah will know what to do.'

'Yes!' said Holly. 'You're right! Come on.'

They ran from the sports centre.

'This way,' said Peter, loping ahead on his long legs, the two girls following close behind.

Miranda, Belinda and Charlotte jumped out of the taxi in the sloping side street by the theatre. Miranda gave the driver some money and they ran to the stage door.

Miranda pushed into the dark vestibule and hammered on the shutter of Ted's office.

'What's all this?' The shutter opened and Ted stared at them. 'You can't come in this way, girls,' he said. 'The show's about to start.'

'We've got to speak to Suzannah,' said Miranda. 'Please, Ted. It's really urgent.'

He saw the anxiety on their faces. 'Is something wrong?' he asked.

'Yes,' said Miranda. 'We haven't got time to explain. Let us through, Ted, please.'

'Go on, then,' said Ted. 'You'll have to be quick. Curtain's up in a few minutes.'

Holding a hand of Charlotte's each, the two girls ran down the long corridors that led to Suzannah Winter's dressing-room.

Without pausing to knock, Miranda flung the door open.

157

The room was deserted. They heard the distant sound of an orchestra starting up.

'We've missed her,' exclaimed Miranda. 'The show's started. She'll be on stage now.'

'We can still take the stuff,' said Belinda. 'Before Gail gets here. At least we can stop her getting to it.'

They went into the dressing-room and closed the door.

Charlotte pulled away from them and knelt down by her mother's make-up case. 'Is Gail a baddie?' she asked, looking up at them.

'A bit of a baddie,' said Belinda. 'But don't worry. The goodies always win.' She crouched beside Charlotte. 'Can you show us where you put it?'

Charlotte nodded and delved her arms deep into the case pushing her mother's things aside. She drew her arms up. Held between her hands was a heavy, clear plastic bag filled with white powder.

'This is it,' breathed Miranda. 'This is the stuff everyone is after.'

'Almost there!' Peter shouted back to Holly. He and Tracy had outstripped her across the open spaces of the gardens, and she was beginning to get a stitch in her side from the long run.

They paused for a moment at the gates, waiting for her to catch up.

Peter pointed along the street. 'That leads almost

158

directly to the theatre,' he said. 'It should only take a couple of minutes.'

Holly nodded, holding her aching side. 'Come on, then.'

The street sloped upwards and Holly was panting heavily as she caught up with the other two at the corner.

She recognised the street. Only a hundred metres away on the other side of the road stood the theatre with its tall signboard above the entrance doors.

A few people were drifting in.

Peter looked at his watch. 'The performance must have just started,' he said. 'I didn't realise we'd been so long.'

They crossed the road.

'Look!' said Tracy. 'It's Gail!'

The young woman was walking rapidly towards the theatre entrance from the opposite side.

'What's she doing here?' said Holly. 'She must know she'll be seen. Suzannah will have the police on to her the moment she spots her.'

'Let's find out,' said Peter.

Gail had run up the steps and had disappeared into the entrance. The three friends ran along the road to the theatre.

An usher barred their way in.

'We need to get in,' Holly said to him. 'We've got to speak to Suzannah Winter.'

The man shook his head. 'No can do,' he said. 'No entry without tickets.'

'We've got tickets!' cried Tracy, feeling in her pocket.

The excitement of the day's discoveries had driven it out of their minds. The tickets that Miranda had given them were for that evening's performance.

The usher examined their tickets with frustrating slowness, but eventually seemed to decide they were real. He stepped aside and the three teenagers entered the foyer.

'It's just started,' the usher called to them. 'Your seats are in the stalls. First door on the left.'

They made their way towards a woman standing in front of closed double doors. She looked at their tickets and opened one of the doors.

'Round to the left,' she told them. 'Row J is about halfway down.' The noise of loud orchestral music burst on their ears as they found themselves in the packed and darkened auditorium.

The stage was a blaze of blue light. Holly recognised the setting from their other visit. It was the Snow Queen's palace, hung with huge icicles, the glistening ice throne dominating centre stage. Suzannah Winter was seated on the throne. As they crept down the side of the theatre, she stood up and began to sing.

'We need to get round to the back,' whispered Tracy, her mouth close to Holly's ear.

Holly nodded. She pointed to an illuminated 'Exit' sign and the three of them moved towards it. They pushed through a curtain into a long corridor.

'Can I help you?' An usher appeared. 'Can't you find your seats?'

'We need to get backstage,' said Holly. 'We're friends of Suzannah Winter.'

The usher shook his head. 'You can't do that,' he said. 'What are you? Autograph hunters? You'll just have to queue at the stage door after the performance.'

Tracy opened her mouth to say something, but Holly stopped her.

'Thanks,' she said. 'Sorry. We'll do that.' She pulled Tracy back through the curtain.

'Why didn't you tell him?' whispered Peter, following them.

'Because we can't afford half an hour trying to explain everything,' said Holly. 'He thought we were after Suzannah's autograph. He's more likely to throw us out than let us backstage.'

People in nearby seats turned to frown at them.

'Be quiet!' someone whispered.

Tracy cautiously drew the edge of the curtain aside. The usher was walking away from them towards the front of the theatre.

'Let me try on my own,' said Tracy. 'They'll never let all three of us through.'

'OK,' said Holly. 'If you see Gail, go and tell Ted. Get him to phone the police.'

'Right,' said Tracy. 'You two stay here.'

She waited for a moment until the usher had turned a corner, then slid into the corridor.

There was a barred door to one side, but it looked like a way out into the street. She debated with herself for a moment. Would it be quicker to go round to the stage door from outside? But there was no certainty that she would be allowed back into the theatre that way.

She shook her head and continued along the corridor until she came to stairs leading up and down. Up, she thought, would only take her to the circle *in the auditorium*. Looking round to check no one was nearby, she slid down the other stairway.

A door barred her way. 'Staff Only'.

She opened the door. The noise of the orchestra was much louder here. She had come to a corridor that led to the orchestra pit. She ran across to another door and came into a dingy hallway that she thought she recognised from her other visit.

She knew that she was now below stage level. If she could only remember the route to Suzannah's dressing-room. She felt sure that Gail would be somewhere near there. Perhaps waiting for Suzannah to come off-stage. Tracy couldn't guess what Gail wanted here, but one thing was certain, Gail hadn't come to watch the performance. She must have some other reason for risking a visit to the theatre, and the only thing that Tracy could think of was that she wanted something from

Suzannah. Something important enough for her to risk everything.

Tracy padded along the deserted corridor, the sounds of the show echoing down from above.

She paused, disorientated by the fact that everything looked half-familiar, but realising she had no real idea of how to get to Suzannah's dressing-room from here.

She had to admit it to herself. She was hopelessly lost.

Miranda knelt down, taking the bag of white powder from Charlotte and weighing it in her hands. She looked at Belinda.

'What do you think?' she said.

'I don't know,' said Belinda. 'But I've seen things that look just like that on the TV news. In reports about the police finding stashes of cocaine.'

'What's cocaine?' asked Charlotte.

'Nasty, bad stuff,' said Miranda. She stood up. 'We'd better get Ted to phone the police,' she said.

The dressing-room door opened.

Gail stood looking at them. Her eyes narrowed as she saw the bag in Miranda's hands. She closed the door behind herself and stood with her back to it.

She reached a hand out, a cold look in her eyes.

'I'll take that,' she said.

12 Tracy in trouble

'Who on earth are you?' A man in black jeans and a black shirt stepped through a doorway and stared at Tracy as she stood, baffled at a T-junction in the corridors under the stage.

Thinking quickly, she gave what she hoped sounded like an embarrassed laugh. 'Am I glad to see you,' she said with a smile. 'I thought I was going to be wandering around down here for ever. Ted sent me to give a message to Suzannah Winter, but I got lost.'

'You certainly did,' said the man. 'But Suzannah will be on-stage now. You won't be able to get any messages to her until the interval.'

'That's OK,' said Tracy. 'I can scribble it down and leave it in her dressing-room.' She smiled hopefully. 'If you can show me which way to go, that is.'

The man gave her the necessary instructions.

'Thanks,' she said. 'You've been real helpful.'

'It might be locked,' he warned her.

'I'll manage,' Tracy called back as she walked rapidly along the corridor in the direction he had indicated.

164

Ha! thought Tracy to herself. *So I've got a brain the size of a walnut, have I, Belinda? I'd like to have seen you talk your way out of that as quickly.*

At last she came to a corridor she really did recognise. There was the door with Suzannah's name-card on it. The key was in the lock.

Glancing round to make sure no one else was about to confront her, Tracy turned the handle and gave the door a push. It opened about half a metre before hitting against something and coming to a jarring halt.

Through the gap she could see the dressing-table with its big mirror. Reflected in the glass she saw Belinda's face. It was obvious from her expression that something was wrong.

Tracy gave the door a hard shove with her shoulder and it sprang wide open. She stared open-mouthed at the scene within. Belinda, Miranda and Charlotte were against the far wall. Gail caught her balance after being pushed forwards by the door, and spun to glare at Tracy, a ferocious expression distorting her face.

'Tracy!' shouted Miranda. 'Catch!'

Tracy's instincts took over. She saw something come hurtling through the air towards her, thrown by Miranda.

Gail grabbed at it but missed. It thudded safely into Tracy's outstretched hands.

'Run!' yelled Belinda.

Tracy had no time to wonder what was going on.

The missile thrown by Miranda was soft and heavy in her hands. Seeing the anger in Gail's face, Tracy snatched the door closed on her and ran.

She knew where she was going now. Towards the stage door. To Ted's office. She glanced down at the package. It had to be the drugs that Charlotte had taken out of the plastic bag. But how had it got there? What had been going on in Suzannah's dressing-room?

There was no time to worry about that now. The important thing was to get to Ted's office and get the police before Gail had the chance to get the package back.

Running into the small entrance lobby, Tracy gave a shout of relief. Standing at Ted's shutter were two uniformed police officers, leaning over and apparently talking to him.

'Quick!' she shouted. 'I've got the . . .' Her voice trailed off as the two heads snapped round and two terribly familiar faces stared at her.

She skidded to a halt.

'Ted!' she yelled. 'They're not the police! Help!' She turned and fled back the way she had come, clutching the package against herself as she ran.

She heard Ted shout something and heard the voices of the man and woman as they came after her.

Tracy had no idea where she was going. She didn't dare run back towards Suzannah's dressing-room for fear of crashing into Gail. She took a different turn and scrambled up a set of stairs, bursting through swing-doors. She found herself in a lofty-walled, cramped area hung with ropes and cluttered with pieces of scenery.

The music from the stage welled out and startled faces turned to stare at her. She was in the wings.

'Stop!' Someone loomed in front of her, arms spread out to halt her. There wasn't a second to try to explain.

She ducked under the flailing arm, striking against a wall that yielded and bounced her forwards, off balance into a group of costumed women at the side of the stage.

She had only a moment to register shocked faces and icy blue costumes as she fell in amongst them and found herself sprawling in a tangle of bodies on the margins of the stage.

'What do we do?' whispered Peter as he and Holly stood against the wall of the auditorium.

'Wait for Tracy to come back,' hissed Holly. 'There's nothing else we *can* do at the moment.' She looked towards the stage.

Suzannah was dressed in her Snow Queen costume, her face chalk-white, her long hair caught up in a tall silvery crown. The icicles that hung from her robes glistened and glinted in the cold blue light as she moved. Music filled the theatre as she sang, alone on stage.

She was singing a sad, lonely song that told of

the years she had spent exiled in her frosty palace with only her ice maidens for company, and of how she longed to go out into the world and find love and friendship.

The music came to a discordant climax as the Snow Queen sank back into her throne with her face hidden in her hands.

The orchestra took up a different, more lively melody, and the Snow Queen lifted her head and looked to the side of the stage.

'My ice maidens,' she called. 'See! Even now they come to me!'

Even at that distance Holly could see that something had happened at the side of the stage which made the Snow Queen stare in surprise.

There were gasps and murmurs from the audience as a couple of dancers in filmy blue costumes came tumbling on to the stage.

There were a few seconds of confusion at the side of the stage as a third dancer fell. For an instant Holly caught a glimpse of familiar blonde hair in the mêlée.

The Snow Queen sat locked in her throne as the dancers picked themselves up. There were a few isolated bursts of laughter from the audience as the dancers rallied themselves and began their dance towards the throne.

Holly grasped Peter's arm. 'That was Tracy,' she whispered. 'Quickly! Something's happened!'

She pushed him through the curtain, glancing

back towards the stage. Tracy's head had only appeared for a split second, and the ice maidens seemed to have pulled themselves together as they danced around the Snow Queen's throne.

Holly and Peter ran down the corridor.

'Gail must have found her,' Holly shouted back. 'We've got to help her.'

They came to the stairs and Holly went pelting down, Peter close behind her. They burst into the corridor that led to the orchestra pit.

'Which way?' panted Peter.

Holly stared round. There were two or three exits.

'This way!' she said, spotting a flight of steps that she thought must lead upwards towards the stage.

Gail grabbed at the dressing-room door as Tracy slammed it closed. She gave a yell of pain as her fingers were caught for an instant in the door jamb and she snatched them free.

Belinda and Miranda ran at her as she clutched at her injured fingers. Belinda brought her shoulder down and crashed headlong into Gail's midriff, hearing a wheeze of expelled air as Gail was knocked against the wall. She felt Gail's strong hands grab at her.

Miranda caught Gail's arm and yanked it with all her strength, pulling her sideways so that legs came up against the edge of a chair and she fell.

Miranda spun round. 'Charlotte!' she shouted. 'Quick! Out!'

They ran for the door, their hands tangling for a moment as both Belinda and Miranda fought to turn the handle.

There was a cry from Gail. Charlotte had stamped down hard on her hand as she had run forwards.

Belinda's fingers closed round the door-handle and she pulled the door open. Miranda swung her arm and caught Charlotte round the waist, scooping her up off her feet and carrying her out through the open door.

They scrambled into the corridor and Belinda brought the door crashing closed.

'Lock it!' shouted Miranda.

Belinda spun the key in the lock. The handle turned, wrenched out of her hand from a grip from inside the room.

They backed away from the door, hearing the frantic sounds of Gail trying to get out.

'It's OK,' gasped Belinda, rubbing her shoulder. 'We've got her.'

'Ted's office!' said Miranda. 'A *phone*!' She hugged Charlotte. 'Are you all right?'

'Yes,' said Charlotte. 'I stamped on her fingers 'cause she's a baddie!'

'That's right,' said Belinda. 'You saved us! Come on!'

They ran to the branch in the corridors that would take them to the doorman's office.

They could hear voices shouting and feet running. There seemed to be a lot of chaos going on towards the side of the stage. They ran the other way, hoping at any moment to see Tracy ahead of them.

'Belinda!' It was Holly's voice. She and Peter came running out of a side entrance.

'We've got Gail locked up!' shouted Miranda. 'And Tracy's got the stuff. It's OK! She's gone this way.' Miranda pointed along the corridor towards the stage door.

'No!' Holly cried. 'Something's wrong. Tracy's gone this way. I saw her.' She pointed towards the stage.

'I'll tell Ted to phone the police,' said Miranda. 'Come on, Charlotte. You come with me.'

The three others stood listening to the shouts from the opposite direction. Suddenly the voices stopped and all they could hear was the music of the orchestra.

Holly ran, turning the corner and pushing through the swing-doors that led to the side of the stage. A small group of people were standing absolutely still in the wings, huddled together, their stunned faces towards a man in a police uniform.

The man was standing with his back to the wall. Holly gave a gasp, recognising the man and seeing in an instant what had silenced the frightened group of people.

He held his arm outstretched towards them. Gleaming dully in his clenched hand was a gun.

Tracy scrambled to her feet, pushing through the milling dancers as they tried to recover from her sudden assault. She stumbled away from the stage, vaguely aware of the dancers running on-stage as hands grabbed for her and pulled her back into the wings.

'Get her out of here!' she heard someone say.

'No!' she cried, struggling. 'You've got to help me.' But the hands held her fast and she was dragged towards the swing-doors.

The doors broke open. The woman in the police uniform stood panting in the doorway.

'Good, you've got her!' she said. 'I'll take her.'

'What's going on?' hissed one of the men who had hold of Tracy. 'There's a performance going on here. What *is* all this?'

'She's wanted,' said the woman, shouldering her way through the people towards Tracy.

'She's not from the police!' shouted Tracy.

The woman's fingers bit into Tracy's shoulder. A confusion of voices rose around Tracy. 'Come on, young lady,' said the woman. She looked round at the startled faces. 'We'll deal with this,' she said.

Tracy saw the bogus policeman run up behind the woman.

She stared round desperately at the other people.

'Help me!' she shouted. 'They aren't the police! They aren't!'

But no one moved to help her.

She kicked out at the woman, scraping the side of her shoe down the length of her shin and stamping hard on her foot. It was an action she had been taught in self-defence classes at school.

The woman gave a shriek of pain and her grip loosened on Tracy's shoulder. Tracy dived sideways between two people and ran backstage.

'Stop her!' shouted the man.

Someone loomed in front of Tracy. No one was going to help her. They all believed the two uniformed people really were from the police. It would only take one person to catch a good hold of her and she'd be handed over to them.

She ducked to avoid the grasping arms. Where could she run to? Where would she be safe?

She spotted a ladder clamped to the wall towards the back of the stage. With a frantic burst of speed she ran to the ladder, shoving the package of deadly white powder down inside her shirt front and leaping for the rungs.

The woman in the police uniform darted forwards, her fingers scraping Tracy's heels as she flung herself up the ladder. Tracy's trailing foot hit against the side of the woman's head and she jerked backwards, away from the ladder.

Tracy climbed.

'Stop right there!' she heard. She glanced down.

The man was pointing towards her, and there was something in his hand.

'He's got a gun!' she heard someone shout.

Someone moved towards the fake policeman and he spun, waving the gun towards them as they backed away.

Tracy hung on to the ladder, not daring to move as the small group of people edged away from the gunman and the woman's hands reached once again for the rungs.

'Come down,' snarled the woman, staring up at her with a deadly look in her eyes. 'Come down, or we'll shoot you down.'

13 Mayhem at the theatre

The sounds from the stage echoed in Holly's ears as she stared at the gun in the man's hand. The performance was carrying on, the actors on-stage unaware of what was happening only metres away from them.

Similarly unaware of what had brought Holly to a halt, Peter nudged past her and was transfixed with shock.

'Get over here,' the man commanded, gesturing with the gun. Wordlessly, Holly and Peter joined the small group of people backstage. As the swing-doors flapped to and fro before becoming still, Belinda saw the gunman and backed out of sight.

Holly looked beyond the man, seeing the woman at the base of the ladder, looking up. Holly followed the line of her eyes and saw Tracy's legs below a hanging section of scenery.

'They're not the police,' said Peter.

'Shut up,' said the man. He flicked a glance over his shoulder. 'Get her!' he said.

Holly saw Tracy's legs disappear upwards as the

woman clung grimly to the lower rungs and began to climb in pursuit.

'What is all this?' One of the men from the group seemed to have gathered his courage. He stepped forwards.

'Get down!' snarled the man in the police uniform, brandishing the gun. 'On the floor. All of you. Now!' His eyes blazed. 'Now!'

The tone of his voice allowed for no argument. The half-dozen or so people in the darkened wings of the stage dropped to the floor.

'Flat!' said the man. 'Lie flat. No one move.'

As Holly lay helplessly on her face it seemed unbelievable that only a few metres away, on a stage blazing with light, the dancers were carrying on the performance without an inkling that there was a dangerous gunman in the theatre, and that above their very heads, Tracy was desperately climbing to escape.

Tracy glanced down. The gulf beneath her made her head swim. She saw the gunman turn to threaten the others and took her chance. If she could get herself up out of sight before he turned towards her again, perhaps she could find some way out of this predicament. After all, the ladder had to lead somewhere.

She climbed rapidly, pushing past hanging ropes. She came up through a narrow wooden platform high above the stage. All about her were the ropes and pulleys that raised and lowered the scenery. A metal gantry stretched out across the stage, meshed with cables and hanging from heavy wires that were attached to beams far above her head. From its underside hung the stage lights, pouring out their cones of blue light down on to the figures that she could see dancing around the Snow Queen's throne.

She looked down through the hole through which she had just climbed. The woman was halfway up the ladder. She was slower than Tracy, but climbing with grim determination up towards her.

Tracy was trapped. There was no escape from here.

Unless . . .

Tracy summoned all her nerve and stepped out on to the gantry. If she could just pick her way across, clinging to the wires that soared up into the darkness of the roof, perhaps there would be another ladder on the far side of the stage.

It was a terrible gamble, but her only other option was to wait there until the woman came up and caught her. And she wasn't going to let that happen if she could help it.

The gantry swayed under her weight.

Don't look down! she told herself as she reached for a taut cable and took another perilous step. There were only narrow strips of metal beneath her feet, and beyond them the seven-metre drop to the stage.

She felt blindly with her foot for a safe purchase on the rocking gantry, staring straight ahead of her through the network of wires and electric cables through which she would have to pass if she were to get safely to the other side.

She could hear nothing above the continuing rhythm of the music. Her shoulder-blades burned as she expected at any moment to feel hands clutch at her.

Go for it, Tracy, she urged herself. The gantry rocked suddenly under her and her foot slipped. She fell, but caught hold of a solid beam of metal.

She looked back. The woman had reached the top of the ladder and climbed on to the gantry behind her. Her face was red with the exertion of her climb, but her eyes were fixed fiercely on Tracy.

Clinging to a cable, the woman suddenly leaned forwards and grasped a tight grip on Tracy's trailing ankle.

Tracy squirmed to get free. She was stretched full-length on the gantry, both hands gripping the metal struts as she tried to pull away from the woman's unrelenting grasp.

As she struggled, Tracy felt the weight of the package slip from inside her shirt.

She let go with one hand, trying to stop the bag from falling. But she was too late. The heavy package of white powder slipped out of her shirt front and fell.

But it didn't fall far. It hit against a lower strip of metalwork and hung sagging over the beam.

The bag was only a few centimetres away from her, and as Tracy gripped the sides of the gantry to save herself from falling, she saw the woman's arm stretch down to retrieve it.

Acutely aware of the perilous fall beneath her, Tracy stretched her leg down and nudged the hanging package away from the woman's groping hand.

With a snarl of rage, the woman caught hold of Tracy's leg again. But this time, Tracy could see from the look in the woman's eyes that she was not simply trying to stop her from getting away.

The woman wrenched at Tracy's leg.

She was trying to pull her off the gantry. She was trying to make her fall.

Backstage, it took Belinda only an instant to register the situation with the gunman. She hadn't been seen by him. She crouched behind the closed doors, listening as Holly, Peter and the others were ordered to the floor.

She had no idea where Tracy was, but she assumed her friend was somewhere backstage, and that the woman was either chasing her or, worse, had already caught her.

Her first thought was to run back to the stage

door office and get help. But Miranda was already doing that. And it could take several minutes for aid to come from that direction.

If Belinda was to help, she would have to do something now. Immediately.

A shout for help would be drowned by the orchestra. And all that would do would be to alert the gunman to her presence.

Then she noticed the glass booth that housed the special effects console.

She crawled across the floor and into the booth. It was empty. The people who should have been in there were amongst those now lying helplessly on the floor under the menace of the gun.

Belinda edged her way silently towards the console, an idea forming in her mind. Maybe, just *maybe*, she could create enough of a diversion to give the others some chance to escape.

She lifted herself to a crouch in front of the console, her eyes scanning over the levers and buttons.

They were arranged in banks. Lighting. Scenery. Stage effects. And other things that she didn't recognise.

She searched for something that would create the maximum of chaos.

She saw a lever that she had been shown before, when they had come into the wings to find Charlotte. The one that she had been told would kick a great flood of dry ice smoke out over the stage. She pulled the lever.

There was a fierce hiss from somewhere behind her, but from this position it was impossible for Belinda to see the results of her action.

Oh, well, she thought. *Better not take any chances.*

She brought her hands hammering down on as many other buttons as she could.

If *this* didn't cause enough mayhem, nothing would!

Holly flung her hands over her head as a colossal crash of thunder echoed out over the stage, followed immediately by a series of blinding lightning flashes. Another deafening rip of thunder burst above her, mingled in with other explosions that sounded like cannons going off.

She glanced up as a thick pall of white smoke came pouring out of a wide funnel only centimetres away from where the startled gunman stood. He vanished into the dense cloud.

Holly scrambled to her feet, hearing screams and shouts from the stage. Pandemonium broke out onstage as the sudden chaos wrought by the special effects brought the performance to a halt.

Holly had no idea what was going on, but it was clear that the deafening noises and the gush of dry ice smoke were not part of the show. In the eddying fog Holly saw figures milling about in confusion.

'Get the curtain down!' she heard someone shout.

Coughing, Holly stumbled to avoid the panicking figures. She had lost track of Peter. All she could see were ghostly figures running through the billowing clouds of dry ice smoke that were engulfing the stage.

White flakes began to cascade down around her as she tried to see what was going on. Something heavy and white came gliding down past her shoulder. The safety curtain had been lowered. She realised that in the impenetrable fog, she had stumbled out on to the stage.

The orchestra came to a chaotic stop and beyond the curtain Holly could hear shouts of confusion and alarm from the auditorium. It had become clear to the audience that something was terribly wrong.

Belinda! thought Holly. It was the only explanation for this sudden explosion of special effects. Belinda had done it, making the effects go haywire in an effort to stop the gunman and his accomplice from catching Tracy.

But where was Tracy? The last Holly had seen of her was her legs disappearing up the ladder as the woman pursued her. Was Tracy somewhere up above the stage, or had she managed to find some escape route? It was impossible for Holly to see from here.

She ran along the front of the stage, her own voice joining the general clamour as she shouted for help.

Out here the dry ice clouds were swirling at waist height, obliterating the stage, but making it possible for Holly to see up above the scenery. Snow was pouring down into her eyes, but she could see the swaying gantry high above the Snow Queen's palace.

She gave a cry as she saw Tracy stretched out on the gantry, struggling as the woman tried to pull her off. Holly stared in horror as Tracy seemed about to fall.

Holly's heart almost stopped as she saw Tracy slide halfway off the gantry. But then Tracy seemed to find a reserve of strength, wrenching her leg out of the woman's hand and pulling herself out of reach.

Even as she shouted encouragement to Tracy, Holly saw the woman reaching downwards, and saw the hanging bag that she was reaching for. Tracy lunged backwards with her hanging leg. Her foot caught the bag, tipping it off the beam and sending it falling towards the stage.

The artificial snow was slippery underfoot as Holly ran under the falling bag, her feet skidding on the stage floor. The bag thudded into her hands, but before she could move she saw a heavy figure come out of the fog.

The gunman was coughing and holding one arm across his eyes. The lightning flashed on and off and more thunder rolled.

At the side of the stage Belinda was hammering her hands down on to the console, wincing at the tremendous noises that were reverberating around her. But was it enough?

She wiped her hand across her forehead, searching the panels for some final piece of chaos.

She gave a triumphant yell and rapidly turned the dial labelled Stage Turntable Control.

With a shout the gunman ran towards Holly. She turned to run, but suddenly the stage slid away from under her and she fell into the mist. The centre of the stage had started to revolve.

Holly rolled and picked herself up, seeing the gunman's arms flailing as he fought for balance on the moving floor.

There was a scream from above her and Holly saw that the woman in the police uniform had slipped from the gantry and was hanging on by her hands, her legs twisting in the snow-filled air.

The gunman let out a shout of rage, falling to his knees, the fog swirling around his chest.

Holly slithered her way to the side of the stage, catching hold of one of the large free-standing icicles that adorned the Snow Queen's palace. The heavy piece of scenery rocked in her arms as she skidded to get round behind it.

She glanced over her shoulder. The gunman was crawling across the floor, and even as she looked he heaved himself to his feet and ran on sliding feet towards her, the gun pointing directly at her, his eyes blazing with anger.

* * *

Tracy had been as shocked as anyone when the first burst of thunder had come bellowing down from the speakers in the roof. She was deafened and blinded as bright lights flashed around her. In the dazzling confusion of light and dark she saw the woman's fingers reach for the bag. And below them she saw the gush of smoke that came out over the stage, bringing the dancers to a chaotic halt.

Taking a firm grip on the gantry bars, Tracy kicked downwards, tipping the bag off its perch and giving a shout as she saw it fall.

The gantry swayed alarmingly on its supporting wires, the pools of blue light flaring out over the spewing mist. Tracy was too occupied with her own troubles to see what was going on down on the stage. All that she knew was that she had got the package out of range of the woman. But now, her thoughts were concentrated on her own escape.

The gantry gave a jerk and a shudder and suddenly the woman slipped over the edge, her hands grabbing to save herself.

Tracy was half-blinded by the thick fall of snow that was pouring from somewhere above her. She crawled the last few metres to the far end of the gantry and hauled herself upright, her heart hammering away in her chest, louder almost than the thunderings and crashings that were battering at her ears.

Clinging on to the supporting wires, Tracy looked down between her feet. She saw Holly run behind the towering, swaying icicle, and saw the gunman moving menacingly towards her.

The rocking tip of the icicle was only a few metres below Tracy. Heavy ropes snaked down from the sides of the stage. If she could swing herself out on to one of them she would only have to climb down a little way. She would be in the perfect position to give the icicle a final kick that would send it crashing on to the stage. Perhaps that would distract the gunman for long enough to allow Holly to escape.

Taking a deep breath, Tracy lunged for a rope. The gantry swung away from beneath her.

She caught the rope in both hands. She screamed as the rope gave in her hands and she felt herself falling.

She swung herself, kicking out wildly with her legs. She was almost upended as her foot caught the point of the icicle.

Her scream turned into a whoop of joy as she pushed down against the icicle and felt it teeter under her weight and begin to fall.

As the rope she was clinging to slowly unwound itself down towards the stage, Tracy saw the huge icicle falling towards the gunman. She saw his hands fly upwards as it tumbled towards him, and saw his gun go spinning away into the thick mist.

Tracy braced herself for a landing as she was

borne safely down the long drop like a spider on its thread.

She landed-waist deep in the mist as Holly came rushing towards her. They caught hold of each other.

'Tarzan!' yelled Tracy. 'Did you see me? Just like Tarzan!'

'I've got the bag!' shouted Holly. 'Are you OK?'

'Yes, I'm fine,' gasped Tracy. 'What about the guy? Did I get him?'

Holly pointed to the man, lying unmoving under the fallen icicle. 'You got him,' she said.

Figures came running towards them out of the sinking fog, Peter amongst them.

'Call the police!' shouted Holly. 'Call the *real* police.'

Shocked faces stared at her.

'We are the police,' said one of the figures that crowded around the two girls. Holly wiped the snowflakes out of her eyes, finally seeing that the man was in uniform. 'What's going on?'

'They were after *this*,' said Holly, holding the bag of white powder up. She grinned and dropped the bag into the policeman's waiting hands. 'We can explain the whole thing, can't we, Tracy? We can explain everything.'

'Oh, wow!' gasped Tracy, sinking to her knees as her legs suddenly collapsed under her. 'I don't know, Holly. I really don't know. This is *some* kind of holiday!'

There was a shout from above.

'She's one of them,' said Peter, pointing upwards to where the other woman was hanging helplessly from the gantry.

The policeman turned and spoke to another officer.

'Go and get her down from there,' he said. He looked in bafflement at Holly. 'And I think you'd better start on your explanation,' he said.

Belinda came running through the dwindling snowfall.

'Are you all OK?' she called.

'Yes,' said Holly. 'Everything's fine. Everything's just fine!'

Peter laughed breathlessly. 'It's just another night out for this lot,' he said. He grinned at Holly. 'There's never any lack of excitement when you're around, is there?'

Holly laughed. 'Just like the old days,' she said.

Peter shook his head. 'Worse,' he said. 'Much worse.'

14 The Snow Queen's party

Applause echoed through the packed auditorium as the music swirled to a climax and the curtain came down. Holly and her friends jumped up from their seats in the stalls, yelling and clapping as the curtain rose again. Suzannah Winter led the cast to the front of the stage.

It was the evening after the ruined showing of the musical, and the Mystery Club, along with Miranda and Peter, were in the stalls. Right in the middle at the front. And this time nothing had happened to prevent a full performance of *The Snow Queen*.

There were five curtain calls before the tumultuous applause died down enough for the cast to leave the stage. Eventually the curtain fell for the final time and the lights in the auditorium went up.

Holly and her friends joined the flood of people heading for the exits.

'Wasn't that the most wonderful thing you've ever seen in your life?' said Tracy. 'I could come and watch it every night for a *month*!'

'*Two* months,' said Miranda. 'I've never seen Suzannah on-stage before. She was brilliant!'

The previous evening had ended with the five friends sitting in Suzannah's dressing-room, explaining to the police everything that they had found out about Gail Farrier and the two fake police officers. The girls had got to Miranda's house late and exhausted – but not too tired to go over the whole story again for Miranda's parents.

They had tumbled into their beds, feeling that they could have slept til noon. Except that Peter was at the door early the next morning to join them for their first day of real, uninterrupted sightseeing around London.

Belinda had finally got to see Horse Guards Parade, and Tracy got her visit to Madame Tussaud's and the Planetarium.

And to crown the day, they found that Suzannah had arranged for them to be given replacement tickets for that evening's performance.

But their surprises weren't over yet.

As they made their way out to the foyer they were approached by a man in evening dress.

'I'm the manager of the theatre,' he said. 'I'd like to have a word with all of you backstage.'

They gave one another puzzled looks.

'I didn't break anything, did I?' asked Belinda, worried that her enthusiastic attacking of the special effects console may have caused some damage.

'No,' said the man. 'It's nothing like that. Come with me.'

He led them back down the long corridor.

As he opened the door to Suzannah's dressing-room there was a burst of applause. The room was packed with people.

Suzannah came forwards with a smile.

'We're having a small party in your honour,' she told them. 'To thank you for all that you've done. And Charlotte's been allowed to stay up late especially to join in.'

Charlotte came running forward, Polly flopping in her arms. 'It's hours past my bedtime,' she said. 'But I'm not sleepy at all.' She took hold of Belinda's hand. 'There's cakes and ice-cream and all sorts of things.'

'Yes, I can see,' said Belinda. Suzannah's dressing-table was laden with food and drink.

Suzannah drew them into the room. 'And there's someone here who'd like a word with you,' she told them.

A man stepped forwards.

'I'm Inspector Todd,' he told them. He smiled. 'A *real* policeman this time.' He shook each of them by the hand. 'I thought you'd like to know the full story.'

'We've already worked it all out,' Holly said with a grin. 'Gail was working for those two crooks, wasn't she? And she tried to double-cross them? That's what started it all.'

'That's exactly what happened,' said the inspector. 'Gail Farrier has confessed everything. Apparently she's been bringing drugs into the country for some time under cover of her couriering work. The two other people were her contacts. Her role was to pass the drugs on to them for an agreed price.'

The inspector smiled. 'But I'm afraid Miss Farrier got greedy. Instead of handing the goods over, she decided she'd try to sell them for herself. Which was when she came unstuck. She thought she would be safe, hiding out at Mrs Winter's house, but she hadn't reckoned on the determination of her two former employers. They found out where she was and set about getting the stuff back off her. Miss Farrier has agreed to give evidence in court to that effect.'

'She should have stuck to dancing,' said Miranda.

'I'm very glad she didn't,' said the inspector. 'Her evidence is going to help us break the entire drugs ring.'

'And it's all because of us,' said Tracy.

'And Charlotte,' added Belinda. 'If Charlotte hadn't taken the key out of the doll they'd have got away with the drugs, wouldn't they?'

'Very possibly,' said the inspector. 'You've all been very helpful. I just wanted to come here and thank you in person for everything you've done. And now,' he continued, looking at his watch, 'I'm afraid I've got to be going. Enjoy your party.'

'Well,' said Miranda, as they made themselves at home with drinks and plates of food, 'I think we've deserved this.'

Belinda sat down with Charlotte on her lap. 'And Charlotte's the guest of honour,' she said.

'I think we should make her an honorary member of the Mystery Club,' said Holly with a laugh.

'And us,' said Miranda. 'What about me and Peter? We ought to be honorary members, too.'

'We can form our own London branch of the Mystery Club,' said Peter.

Tracy shook her head. 'No way. You're not allowed to solve any mysteries without us,' she said.

'OK,' said Miranda. 'If we ever spot anything mysterious, we'll give Holly a ring and you can all come down and stay again.'

'Oh, no,' said Belinda. 'Next time I come down to London it's going to be for a proper holiday. We get enough mysteries back home, thank you very much.' She gave Charlotte a hug. 'You don't want any more mysteries do you, Charlotte?'

The little girl opened a sleepy eye. 'Polly says she likes mysteries,' she murmured. 'She wants to be in the Mystery Club, too.'

Holly laughed. 'I suppose it's only fair,' she said. 'After all, she was right in the middle of this one.'

'And she's probably brighter than Tracy,' grinned Belinda.

'And less lazy than you,' said Tracy.

Miranda gave one of her shrieks of laughter. 'Don't you two ever stop?' she asked.

Belinda laughed. 'Only when we're asleep,' she said.

Holly lifted her glass. 'A toast,' she said. 'To Polly the doll, the newest member of the Mystery Club.'

The five friends drained their glasses.

'And now,' said Belinda. 'As I'm busy keeping Charlotte comfortable, would someone like to get me something to eat? After all, this is supposed to be a party.'

'Belinda, tell me a story?' murmured Charlotte.

'Of course,' said Belinda. 'What sort of story would you like? A fairy story?'

Charlotte lifted her head. 'No,' she said. 'A *mystery* story.'

'Oh, no,' laughed Peter. 'Not *another* mystery.'

'Why not?' said Holly, smiling. 'There's no shortage of those sort of stories while the Mystery Club is around!'

BURIED SECRETS

by Fiona Kelly

Holly, Belinda and Tracy are back in the
eighth thrilling adventure in the
Mystery Club series, published by
Knight Books.

Turn the page to read the first chapter . . .

1 Digging up a story

'What is it? What's happened?' Tracy came bursting into the classroom where Holly and Belinda were sitting. 'Jamie said you needed me urgently. I came right away.'

Holly smiled at her. 'It wasn't *that* urgent,' she said. Tracy was dressed in her tennis kit. It looked like she'd run all the way from the school tennis courts.

Belinda laughed, looking at Holly through her wire-framed spectacles. 'I told you it would work,' she said.

It had been Belinda's idea to send Holly's younger brother, Jamie, out in search of Tracy.

'What would work?' Tracy said suspiciously. 'This had better be good,' she said.

Holly held a pen poised over the Mystery Club's red notebook. 'I need some help,' she said. 'I can't think of anything to write for the next issue of the school magazine, and Steffie wants something by early next week.'

'*What*?' yelled Tracy. 'You can't be serious! I was thrashing Jenny Fairbright two sets to love, and you drag me all the way over here for *that*? To help you write an *article*?' I thought you were in some kind of trouble.'

'I am,' said Holly. 'If I miss Steffie's deadline I'm going to look really stupid, especially as I promised her something special this time.'

If Holly had a rival at the Winifred Bowen-Davies School, it was Steffie Smith, the editor of *Winformation*, the school magazine.

'But I was *winning*!' exclaimed Tracy. 'I was beating the school champion.'

'It's only a game,' said Belinda with a yawn. 'Anyway,' she said with a grin, 'too much exercise is bad for you – I read it somewhere.'

'Then you've got nothing to worry about,' said Tracy. 'If being a lazy, idle lump is good for you, you should live to be a hundred.'

'Do you two think you could put the personal abuse on hold for a while?' said Holly. She looked up at Tracy. 'I'm sorry about messing up your game, but this *is* important. You know what Steffie's like. She'd just love to get one over on me. I've really got to think of something brilliant for the magazine.'

'Did I hear the word brilliant?' called a voice from the doorway. 'Are you talking about me?'

'I can't say the word "brilliant" and the name "Kurt Welford" have ever been linked in my mind,' said Belinda, as Kurt came into the room.

Kurt grinned. He was used to Belinda's sense

of humour. Tall and blond, his main link with the Mystery Club was as Tracy's part-time boyfriend.

He smiled at Tracy. 'I thought you were spending your lunch-break playing tennis?' he said. 'What happened?'

'This pair happened,' said Tracy. 'Would you believe they dragged me all the way over here to help them come up with an article for the school magazine?'

'What sort of article do you want?' asked Kurt.

'If I knew that I wouldn't be sitting here with a blank page in front of me,' Holly said impatiently.

'What about something on cricket?' suggested Kurt. 'I could help write it.'

Belinda yawned again. 'Fascinating,' she said. 'People could read it last thing at night as a cure for insomnia.'

'I suppose you'd prefer something on horses?' said Kurt.

'That's a thought,' Belinda said brightly. 'We could do an interview with Meltdown.'

'No it isn't,' Holly said firmly. 'For heaven's sake, you lot, isn't *anything* interesting going on around here?'

'There's that dig over at Hob's Mound,' said Kurt. He gave Belinda a cool smile. 'But I don't suppose you'll want to hear about that.'

'What dig?' asked Holly. 'Digging for what?'

'Buried treasure,' said Kurt. 'So I've heard, anyway.'

'Ignore him,' said Belinda. 'He's winding us up.'

'Am I?' said Kurt. 'I needn't bother telling you all about it, then, if it's not really happening.'

'Take no notice of Belinda,' said Holly. 'Come on, Kurt, let us in on it. What's going on?'

'The university has set up an archaeological dig at Hob's Mound,' explained Kurt. 'Do you know the place?'

'I do,' said Tracy. 'It's out west of here, isn't it?'

'That's right,' said Belinda. 'It's just a big grassy lump in the middle of a field. Isn't there some story about it being haunted or something?'

Kurt nodded. 'That's the place. You can tell it's not a natural part of the countryside by the shape of it.' He described a smooth dome in the air with his hand. 'Sitting there in the middle of all these flat fields. They've known for ages that it was a Celtic burial mound. Now they've got hold of some new evidence that suggests someone pretty important might be buried in there. Some Celtic chieftain or other. So the university has funded a new excavation.' Kurt smiled round at the three girls. 'And they started digging this morning.'

Holly wrote 'Hob's Mound' in her notebook. 'Hold on, though,' she said. 'How come you know all about this? It hasn't been in the papers.'

Kurt grinned. 'Not yet it hasn't,' he said. 'But don't forget, my dad is editor of the *Express*. He gets all this sort of information before everyone else. And he's asked me to go over there this afternoon to take some photos.'

'We could have a real scoop here,' said Holly. 'Think of the headlines: "Schoolgirls help to find ancient buried treasure".'

'Ancient, mouldy, horrible old bones, you mean,' said Tracy. 'Where does the treasure come into it?'

'Don't you know *anything*?' said Belinda. 'In ancient times when they buried someone important they always surrounded them with gold and jewels and stuff like that.' She looked at Kurt. 'That's right, isn't it?'

Kurt nodded. 'There could certainly be some interesting things in there.'

Tracy gave Kurt a thoughtful look. 'And they reckon all this stuff is still going to be in there, after all this time?'

'That's the idea,' said Kurt. 'With any luck I'm going to get a photo of them finding something amazing. I hope so, anyway. I'm going straight over there from school this afternoon.'

Holly grinned at her friends. 'In that case,' she said, 'I think we ought to go with you. Steffie Smith will be *green* if we come back with the scoop of the century.'

'Is that settled, then?' said Tracy. 'Can I get back to beating the living daylights out of Jenny Fairbright now, or is there something *else* you desperately need me for?'

'You could nip up to the canteen and get me a

couple of sandwiches,' said Belinda, staring down at the empty chocolate wrapper. 'I'm starving.'

'Dream on,' said Tracy. 'Get your own sandwiches – you could do with the exercise. Coming over to the tennis courts with me, Kurt?'

'We'll meet outside after school,' called Holly as Tracy and Kurt headed for the door. 'Don't be late.'

'Well?' said Belinda to Holly after the others had gone. 'Are you happy now you've got something lined up for the magazine? Can we get back to something a bit more important now?'

'Like what?' asked Holly.

'Like getting over to the ice-cream parlour before the end of break,' said Belinda, heaving herself up.

The two girls headed for the school gates, Holly's mind already working on an opening sentence for her article: 'Important archaeological finds discovered near Willow Dale. Your reporter, Holly Adams, was at Hob's Mound as the ancient site was opened up for the first time in over a thousand years.'

Yes, she thought, *That* would shut Steffie Smith up once and for all. Especially if Kurt was right, and the Hob's mound turned out to be full of priceless antiquities.

She could hardly wait.